HEY, DICK AND DOM, HAVE YOU SEEN THE TIME?

Look at the time!

THE KIDS WERE ALL HERE AT TWENTY TO NINE!

Shout!

SO DON'T BE SURPRISED IF YOU HEAR THEM SHOUT,

"YOU'VE BOTH GOT YOUR TROUSERS ON INSIDE OUT!"

Freestyle!

GO, GO, DICK AND DOM IN DA BUNGALOW!

GO, GO, DICK AND DOM IN DA BUNGALOW!

GO!

CALLING ALL BUNGALOWHEADS!

DICK: "How does it feel to be between the covers, Dom?"
DOM: "It feels lovely - all snug and toasty like Wee Willy Winky on his night off."
DICK: "NOOO, I meant 'how does it feel to be between the covers of a BOOK?' you muppet!"
DOM: "Oh, yes - brilliant! I read a book once! The Nanny Nob Nob's Book of Records."
DICK: "What was it like?"
DOM: "It was like two pieces of card with some paper in between. With stuff on the paper like words and pictures and a fly that I squashed inside by accident. Our book will be much better though."
DICK: "Yes it will! I'm pretty amped about it already. How excited are you that we've got a book with our names on it?"
DOM: "I'm so excited, I've just got to let it out."

DOM: "Aaah, that's better. And it reminds me - I can't understand why they didn't make it a scratch 'n' sniff book."
DICK: "I think you just answered your own question there, mate. That smells worse than one of Nanny Nob Nob's runny buffets. Have you been at that jar of pickled eggs again?"
DOM: "No, just last night's pizza."
DICK: "You had cold pizza for breakfast?"
DOM: "Yes."
DICK: "Wait a minute, though...we didn't have pizza last night."
DOM: "We didn't?"
DICK: "No."
DOM: "Ah...then I think I'm going to be..."
DICK: "Urgh! Not again! Let's end this page here and get on with the contents..."

CONTENTS

Enter da Bungalow!

BING BONG!

DIS IS DA BUNGALOW

People with a low tolerance to shrill, squeaky voices are advised not to open this cupboard. Come to think of it, no one is advised to open this cupboard.
That's Dom's Mum ringing to remind him to change his pants.
BRRRINGGG!
This is Dick's domestic science project turned biology experiment. The pan's been here so long it's developed its own ecosystem.
What did Dick say when he saw that someone had eaten his secret biscuit stash? "Crumbs!"
The cooker – useful for mushing peas, baking beans and cooking up batches of Creamy Muck Muck.

If you want to be a Bungalowhead, first you've got to know da Bungalow. So here's everything you ever wanted to know – plus some stuff you'll wish you didn't.
People carrying sausages are not advised to enter the attic.
People always ask me how I get my antlers to stand up like this. So tell them – I use plenty of moose!
What do you think of this sofa, Dick?
Rubbish!
This is where Dom spilt his banana custard.

more of DA BUNGALOW

The skeleton wanted to go to a party – but he didn't have any body to go with.

Here's Nanny Nob Nob's book of recipes. It contains all the ingredients for a nice pie – and that's just the bogies that Dom has wiped on the cover.

Secret snot bucket – no one 'nose' it's here!

LUMPY TRUMPS

This is the toilet. Watch out for the Turtle's Head!
What's brown and goes up and down?
Poo on a pogo stick?
No! Gravy in the elevator!
This is where Dick left his half-eaten Scotch egg.

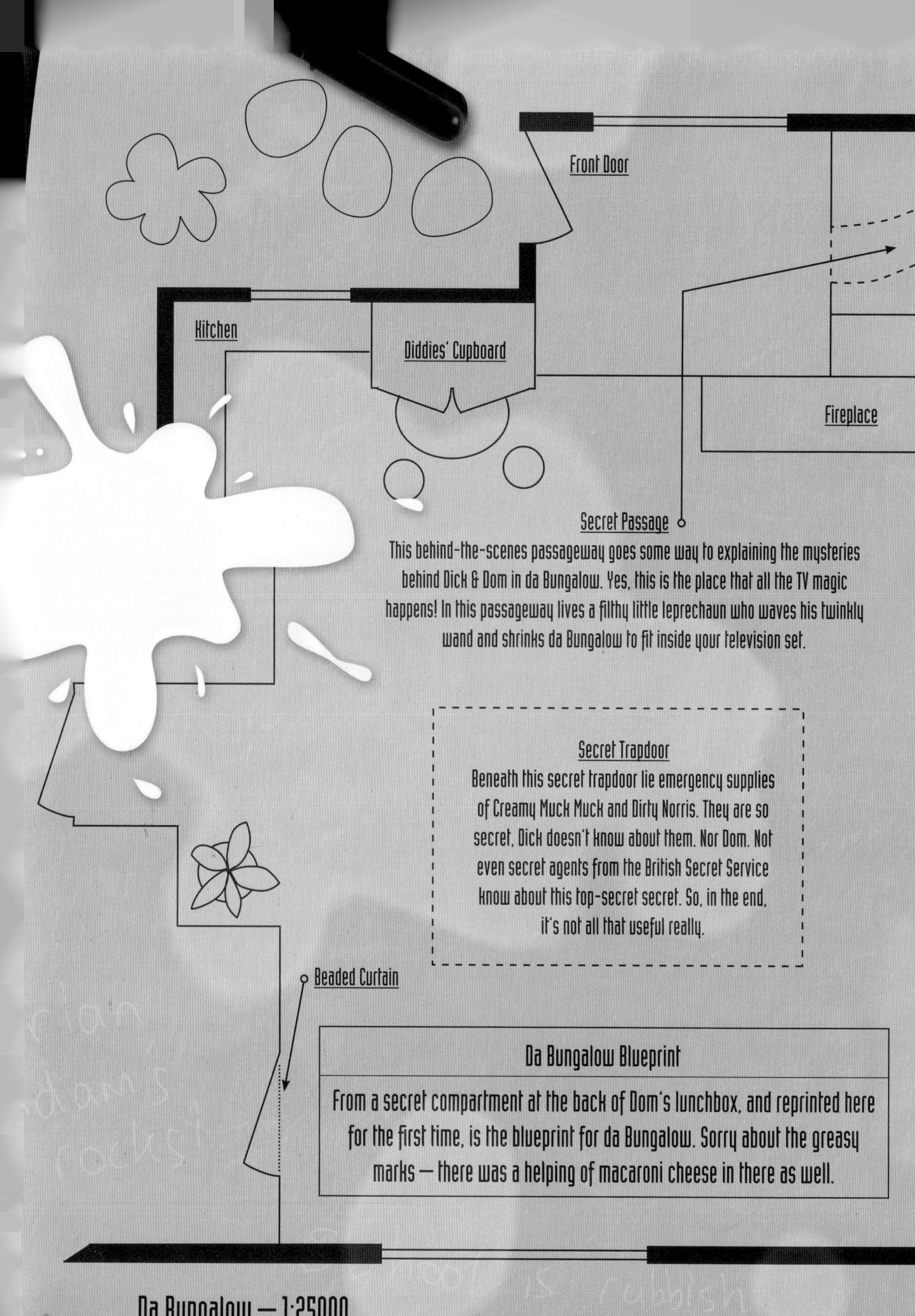
Front Door
Kitchen
Diddies' Cupboard
Fireplace
Secret Passage
This behind-the-scenes passageway goes some way to explaining the mysteries behind Dick & Dom in da Bungalow. Yes, this is the place that all the TV magic happens! In this passageway lives a filthy little leprechaun who waves his twinkly wand and shrinks da Bungalow to fit inside your television set.
Secret Trapdoor
Beneath this secret trapdoor lie emergency supplies of Creamy Muck Muck and Dirty Norris. They are so secret, Dick doesn't know about them. Nor Dom. Not even secret agents from the British Secret Service know about this top-secret secret. So, in the end, it's not all that useful really.
Beaded Curtain
Da Bungalow Blueprint
From a secret compartment at the back of Dom's lunchbox, and reprinted here for the first time, is the blueprint for da Bungalow. Sorry about the greasy marks – there was a helping of macaroni cheese in there as well.
Da Bungalow – 1:25000

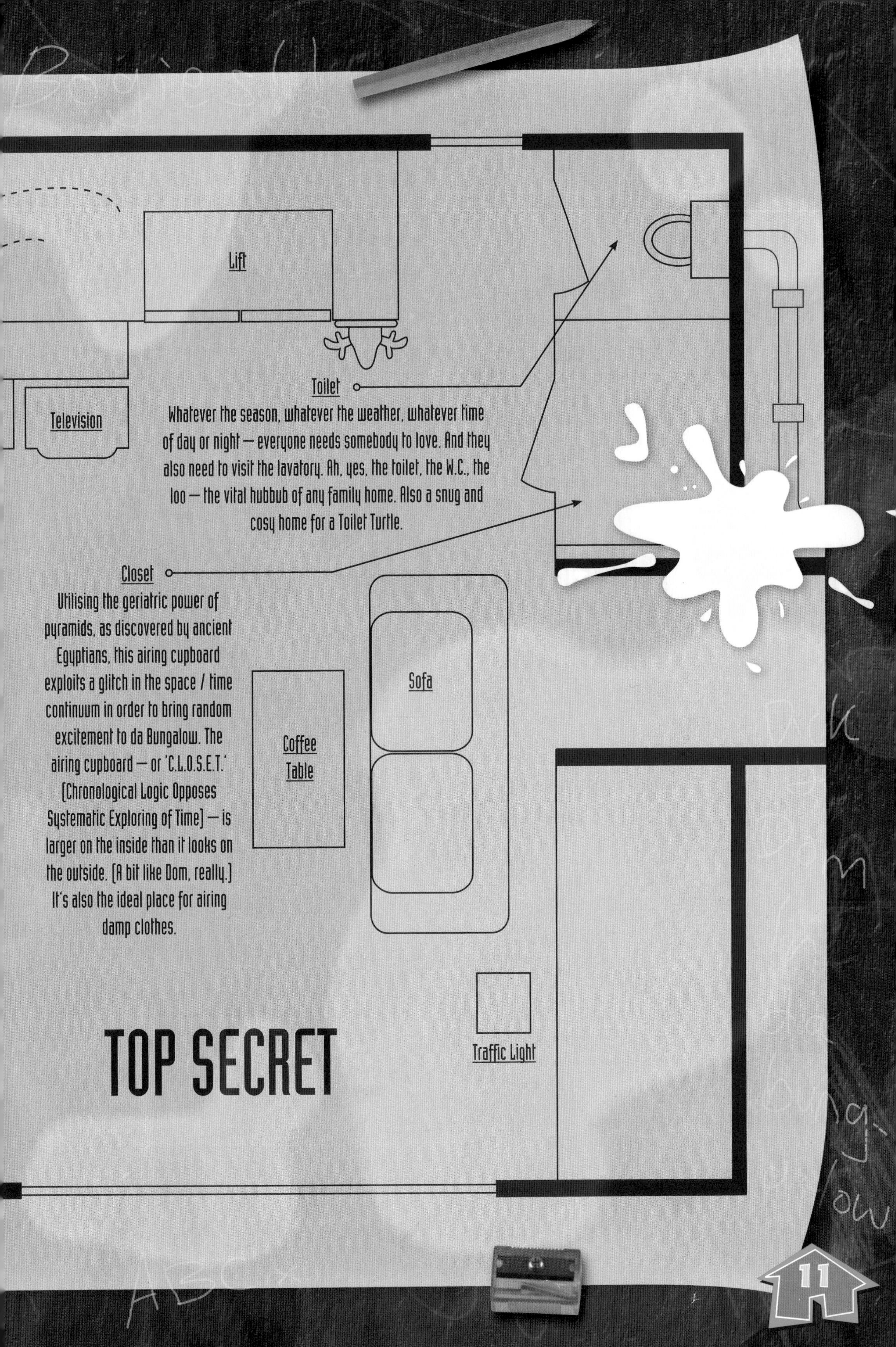
Lift
Television
Toilet
Whatever the season, whatever the weather, whatever time of day or night – everyone needs somebody to love. And they also need to visit the lavatory. Ah, yes, the toilet, the W.C., the loo – the vital hubbub of any family home. Also a snug and cosy home for a Toilet Turtle.
Closet
Utilising the geriatric power of pyramids, as discovered by ancient Egyptians, this airing cupboard exploits a glitch in the space / time continuum in order to bring random excitement to da Bungalow. The airing cupboard – or 'C.L.O.S.E.T.' (Chronological Logic Opposes Systematic Exploring of Time) – is larger on the inside than it looks on the outside. (A bit like Dom, really.) It's also the ideal place for airing damp clothes.
Sofa
Coffee Table
Traffic Light
TOP SECRET

Dick's Glossary of Bungalow-isms

Congratulations! You've reached page 12 without having to refer to the glossary! A glossary is not a shiny foodstuff but a guide to all the words you need to understand this book. So go ahead and learn how to speaka da lingo da Bungalow!

Bad: Good. Also, bad.

Baked beans: My favourite food – nice to eat, even better squished between your hands.

Bogies: Dom's favourite food. No, not really! Bogies is a game we take very seriously. We take it in turns to say "bogies", starting quietly and getting gradually louder. Bogey volume is measured on the snot-o-meter. The first person to chicken out is the loser! Remember, bogies is hard enough for trained professionals like us… but even easier for you!

Bungalow: The single-storey house where we live which, mysteriously, also has an attic and a cellar.

Bungalow Battle Bots: Bots that battle in da Bungalow. Did I really have to explain that?

Bungalow Boffins: Big-eared kids that make up games for us to play.

Bungalow gold: Classic moments from our TV show, of which there are a great many.

Bungalowhead: Anyone that likes the stuff we like!

Creamy Muck Muck: Icky white stuff that we like to tip over our heads.

Custard: A sweet sauce ideal with fruit puddings – but even better put in bins and squelched between your toes.

Da: The. I would like to personally apologise to English teachers everywhere for that one. We do not mean to keep making such a silly mistake all of da time.

Diddly squit: Nothing. Nada. Zero. Zilch. Zip. Get used to it!

Diddy Dick and Dom: Smaller, squeakier and stinkier, versions of your very own hosts. They live in the pink cupboard by the kitchenette.

Dirty Norris: Icky brown stuff that we like to tip over our heads.

Little Bob Peep: A strange chap with a penchant for stick-on beards and bonnets. Very good at wrestling, despite his appearance to the contrary. Looks a bit like Dom…

Martin Floppy Horns: Mysterious Viking with a face of stone. You can't make him laugh – but you can try! Looks a bit like me…

Mushy peas: Peas that have been cooked so long they have become mushy. It's that simple. We love eating them because they make us f… feel full up!

Nanny Nob Nob: A Nanny of whom we are very fond. She is a wonderful, wise woman... who smells sausagey.

Pants: Rubbish. Bad.

Pants Dance: A dance that is not at all rubbish or bad. Confusing, isn't it?

Prize Idiot, The: The man who lives next door to us. He isn't very bright. In fact, he's an idiot – but we prize him for it.

Snot: Icky green stuff that we like to… ah, you must be getting the picture by now!

SHUUUT UUUP!: A not very nice way of saying, "Please, be quiet."

Tom Dickunharry: Red-faced auctioneer in a brown coat and flat cap. (He looks eerily like Dick.)

Turtle's head, The: The turtle that lives in the toilet. Doesn't look like me, luckily!

Undercrackers: underpants.

How Much of a BUNGALOWHEAD are you?

1. How often do you change your underwear?

- Every day.
- Every couple of days.
- Once a week.
- What underwear?

2. What would you say is your best feature?

- Your naturally curly hair.
- Your charming laugh.
- Your gobsmackingly dirty fingernails.
- Your size 16 feet.

3. What are your hobbies?

- Collecting bogies – you have some that aren't even yours.
- Playing ping pong – primarily pong.
- Dancing – especially with pants on your head.
- Pony riding, penfriends and practising first aid.

4. What's your greatest talent?

- Your ability to burp at will.
- You're great at making people laugh.
- You're too modest to say, but your Nan says you have a beautiful singing voice.
- That thing you can do with your tongue that makes people go, "Eeeew!"

5. What would you say is your most unappealing habit?

- Picking your nose.
- Biting your nails.
- Biting your toenails.
- Sometimes you can be a little bossy.

6. What's your greatest ambition?

- To be President of your local Badminton Club.
- To be Prime Minister – so you can create more holidays.
- To get twelve gobstoppers in your mouth at the same time.
- To be the first Prime Minister to get twelve gobstoppers in your mouth at the same time.

Mostly
Have you learned nothing from Dick and Dom? Keep reading this book and don't stop – not even to wash your hands – until you get to the end.

Mostly
Not bad! If you were a Dick and Dom plant, you'd be a little seedling. Keep watching da Bungalow and you may grow into a big stinky tree.

Mostly
Well done, you! You certainly know your Dirty Norris from your Creamy Muck Muck! And now you can enjoy the rest of this book with a smug grin on your mush!

Mostly
You're bad...too bad! Even Dick and Dom would be ashamed to be seen out with you! But, hey, look on the bright side – you're not the Prize Idiot. Are you?

Don't be BORED play these GAMES

Dick and Dom are never bored because they're always making up brilliant things to do. Next time you and a mate are at a loose end, why not try pulling off one of these pranks and games – all tried and tested by Dick and Dom themselves!

This is the News!

Good evening, my name is Richard McCourt and I'm here with the evening's news... The Prime Minister astounded colleagues at the Labour Party Conference today by letting rip with a real trouser shaker in the middle of his speech about the state of school dinners. He blamed it on the cauliflower cheese and baked beans he'd eaten at lunch.

You only need a couple of mates around to play this and have a real laugh. Write a fake news report. Get a friend to read it out – straight-faced, no laughing! – in a newsreader style.

WHAT'S UP?

Next time you're out with a mate, stand in the middle of an open area – like a shopping centre or a sports field. Start looking up at the sky and then point at something. In about a minute or so you will have lots of people looking up at the sky and wondering what's going on. Then...just leave! You can always come back later and see if anyone's still looking up!

THE HARDEST WALK!

Try playing this game with a gang of mates. The first person to go has to walk from here to there (anywhere) in a very silly way. Remember to move your arms, head, butt and everything - not just your legs! And try saying something silly as well - sing, yodel, shout, whatever! The next person to go has to do the same thing, copying everything as much as possible - the walk, the movement, the voice... The third person copies the second person and so on until you lose the plot completely!

Ollie ollie oxen feee!
Wickity wickity woo!

SNEEZY JET!

Tip a little water into your hand. Then fake a sneeze and flick your hand while going up to 'cover your sneeze.' Your friend will think the water has flown out of your nose - but 'snot' really!

READING, WRITING... ARMADILLO!

Think of a silly-sounding word that makes you laugh. Then read something out loud: a school textbook; a story; a song; anything! Every time you see a word beginning with the same letter as your silly-sounding word, then use your word instead. If you like, you can make it into a game. If you forget to use your silly word then a mate can stop you and carry on from where you left off. The quicker you read or sing, the harder it is!

If your silly word was "dribble," and you sang the Dick and Dom theme tune, it would go like this...

Wake up dribble and dribble and get out of bed, Get yourself dribble there's a crazy dribble ahead...!

BA-DOINGG!

Dead simple this one! Leave your bedroom door ajar, and balance a cushion on top of the door. Call a mate into your room and when they push open the door...they get a cushion on their head! Ba-doingg!

WILD ANIMAL ATTACK!

Next time you're in the park or school playing fields, shout, "Arrrgh! Lions!" And then, when you've got everyone's attention, point to the ground and say, sweetly, "Dandelions!"

GET KNOTTED!

Try this joke on a pesky brother or sister. Turn their jumpers inside out and tie knots in the sleeves. Turn them back the right way and hang them up. Make sure you're around when they put their jumper on for guaranteed laughs!

Mystic Dick

Will it be chips or jacket spuds? Will it be salad or frozen peas? Will it be mushrooms or fried onion rings? You'll have to wait and see what's for dinner, but Mystic Dick will do his best to reveal everything else.

AQUARIUS: JAN 20 – FEB 18
Venus and Pluto are in your sign. Venus means drinking fizzy pop and jumping up and down to McFly. Pluto means you may throw up. Guffscope: A mate's pants are riding low – remember to keep pulling them up on this matter.

PISCES: FEB 19 – MAR 20
There is a full moon on the horizon and Uranus is in ascendancy. If you're going swimming, make sure to tie the string in your swim shorts. Guffscope: The sun in your sign gives you a nice warm feeling. I think it's the sun, anyway.

ARIES: MAR 21 – APR 19
Your moods are up and down like a yo-yo. Your head is like a spinning top. Your finances are all snakes and ladders. Do you live in a toyshop, or what? Guffscope: You're going to benefit from a windfall – your own or that of someone else.

TAURUS: APR 20 – MAY 20
Your energy levels are low! Pump them up by making sure you eat a healthy, balanced diet – with plenty of beans and bran – and then join an aerobics group. Guffscope: Remember – clean pants, clean thoughts!

GEMINI: MAY 21 – JUN 21
Jupiter means travel and it's in your sign. So if you've broken something recently – such as wind, for example – then just move away from the scene of the crime. Guffscope: Eat your greens and you'll always turn up trumps!

CANCER: JUN 22 – JUL 22
In private you show a serious, authoritative side. In public you act like a big, silly girl. What's up with that? Guffscope: Changes are afoot – and while you're putting on clean socks, how about changing your pants?

LEO: JUL 23 – AUG 22
You have a lot on your mind at the moment. Perhaps it's time for a haircut. Or just take off that hat. Guffscope: Nebulous Neptune forms a mist over social affairs – so perhaps you ought to think about staying at home.

VIRGO: AUG 23 – SEPT 22
If you think something bad is in the air – have the courage to walk away from it. That way, no one will think to blame you. Guffscope: All is not what it seems. Someone really did just make an egg sandwich in the kitchen.

LIBRA: SEPT 23 – OCT 22
Mars means conflict and it's in your sign. So think about not borrowing your sisters' dolls to practise radical makeovers. Guffscope: All that glimmers is not gold. Especially if you've been eating glitter again.

SCORPIO: OCT 23 - NOV 21
Listen to your inner voice. Unless it tells you to do bad things – and then it's probably best you just ignore it. Guffscope: Invisible forces are at work – but your nose will help you sniff out the culprit.

SAGITTARIUS: NOV 22 – DEC 21
Be careful if you're making a journey – a full moon in Virgo is going to put a spoke in your wheel. Or it could be that big boy from down the road. Guffscope: If you have lost something recently, it's probably where you left it.

CAPRICORN: DEC 22 – JAN 19
You're going to meet a mate walking his dog. Talk to him – but make sure you don't put your foot in it. Guffscope: You're riding high on a wave of popularity, but it might be short-lived thanks to an ill wind blowing your way.

PUERILE POO POEM

What's so funny about poo?
It doesn't make ME laugh. Does it you?
I mean, we all have to go to the loo,
So what's so funny about poo?

Some people think we should keep it in,
And that makes me want to shout:
"We all wee and we all poo,
So come on and let it out!"

Poo poo poopy poo,
Poo-poo poo-poo poo,
Ploppy poo and wee-wee too,
I'M DEFINITELY not laughing. Are you?

What's so funny about poo?
I'm still not laughing. Are you?
I have to poo, and you do too,
So what's so funny about poo?

Some people think it's rude to say it,
Like Grannies, Mums and Aunts,
But they all wee and they all poo,
And they all wear great big pants.

Poo poo poopy poo
Poo-poo poo-poo poo
Ploppy poo and wee-wee too
I'm so TOTALLY not laughing.
I'm just not. No way.
It's not funny.
And this is the end.
Because this is the bottom of the page.
Oooh! I said "bottom"! Ha ha ha ha ha...

Remember! Writing poems about poo is neither big nor clever...

Brown sticks float over,
Rapidly moving water,
I THINK they are sticks!

DOM'S ~~TOP~~ bottom TENS

The first warm winds of spring blowing across the land are not always remarked upon – but there's no need for such events to go unheralded! Let Dom explain the subtle difference between ordering fries in the school dinner queue and drying wet clothes during assembly.

Dom's ten funniest things to say after letting one rip.

"Would you like fries with that?"

"Anyone for air hockey?"

"Timber!"

"Taxi for Mr Brown!"

"Fore!"

"You sunk my battleship!"

"Thar she blows!"

"Shiver me timbers!"

"That's torn it!"

"Bad dog!"

RIPPTER SCALE

How bad was your guff on a scale of one to ten? Use the Rippter Scale to find out...

1 | 2

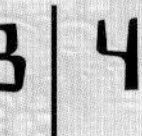

Rippter Scale rating... 1
Volume... Inaudible.
Wind factor... A warm feeling.
Effect... Makes the dog whine.

Rippter Scale rating... 2
Volume... A pin drop.
Wind factor... A gentle breath.
Effect... Makes your kid sister blush.

3 | 4

Rippter Scale rating... 3
Volume... Quiet as a mouse.
Wind factor... A prolonged sigh.
Effect... Makes your big sister elbow you in the ribs and hold her nose.

Rippter Scale rating... 4
Volume... Whisper in the grass.
Wind factor... A light, southerly breeze.
Effect... Makes your parents groan and start opening windows.

Dom's ten ~~worst~~ best places to break wind.

In a packed lift.

While wearing ballet tights.

In an exam – unless it's a flan baking exam and then no one will notice.

In an art gallery.

During a music recital – unless you're sitting in the brass wind section, and then you might just get away with it.

In the school dinner queue.

In the headmaster's office.

In a swimming pool.

During assembly.

In your sleeping bag.

5 | 6

Rippter Scale rating... 5
Volume... A gentle murmur.
Wind factor... Strong enough to ruffle hair.
Effect... Makes your Granny faint.

Rippter Scale rating... 6
Volume... Loud enough to turn heads.
Wind factor... Sufficient to dry wet clothes.
Effect... Turns milk sour.

7 | 8

Brrrrruurrp!!!

Rippter Scale rating... 7
Volume... Mobile ringtone.
Wind factor... Great for flying kites.
Effect... Gets you expelled from Brownies.

Rippter Scale rating... 8
Volume... Trumpet voluntary.
Wind factor... Door rattling.
Effect... Blows away cobwebs.

9 | 10

Rippter Scale rating... 9
Volume... Heavy rock guitar solo.
Wind factor... Window shaking.
Effect... Empties the room/office/bus/aeroplane

Rippter Scale rating... 10
Volume... Jet engine.
Wind factor... Gale force.
Effect... Propels you forwards at thirty miles an hour – from a standing start.

THE BOGEY MOON

JANUARY ?????

BRINGING YOU THE FILTHIEST STORIES

VOLUME NO. 4 567 897

THE DICK STORY

NOT TRUE

Who is the enigma known not only as Dick, but also Richard McCourt, son, best mate and "Oi! You off the telly!"? Let's find out more.

Richard Henman Tennis McCourt was born in a barn at the age of seven months and has never closed a door in his life. Before he became a master of the televisual arts, Dick tried his hand at various artistic pursuits.

At the age of two, he was a stand-up comedian, touring the hard Working Men's Clubs of South West Norris as "Baby-faced Dick – you'll laugh 'til he cries!"

The pressures of touring were too much for a toddler, however, and Baby-faced Dick was put into retirement at the tender age of five. With all this extra time on his hands, Dick turned his attentions to playing with toy soldiers and trying to ride a bike without stabilisers. In no time at all, he became an expert in both these fields and he was able to become a normal school boy.

Dick was a grade A (for average) student. But nothing could stop the stars that twinkled in this boy's eyes! At the age of 18, Dick dazzled a Professor at his University interview by performing Rachmaninoff's *Prelude in C-sharp minor* – on a melodica.

Studying at Footlights College, Muckbridge, he wrote plays for his fellow students including *Much Ado About Norris*, *Muckbeth* and *A Midsummer Night's Creamy Muck Muck*.

His most successful play, however – the one that would gain him worldwide notoriety, if not critical acclaim – was *Muckeo & Norrisette*. A musical satire on a television chat show, the piece contained 8,000 references to muck and three hundred uses of the word Norris.

The follow up – *Muckeo & Norrisette Do America* – was a greater success with critics who loved the story of a Danish Prince seeking revenge for the mucking up of da palace Bungalow. *...Do America* also gave the world the first glimpse of the character that was to make Dick a household name – Muckstaff. A rotund and rosy-faced fellow, Dick played the part of Muckstaff himself – under very heavy make-up.

He played the part for umpteen years until the pressure of putting a duvet up his jumper and yelling "Yo ho, me hearties!" before keeling over every night (and twice on a Saturday) simply became too much. Dick left the business of show to rear Toilet Turtles and build up his collection of naval fluff.

Dick & Dom In Da Bungalow brought Dick out of a long period of retirement and he's grateful for the work. In his own words, "I count every show as a gift – not a given. Every viewer I get is a blessing for someone who thought they had thrown their last bucket of Muck years ago."

Exclusive

Dick's Bag

Get closer to Dick than his pants with this amazing Scoop – a rummage around inside his bag! See what the only person called Dick who lives in da Bungalow can't live without – and maybe some of his star quality will rub off on you! Like body glitter. Or Spilt Spaghetti Sauce.

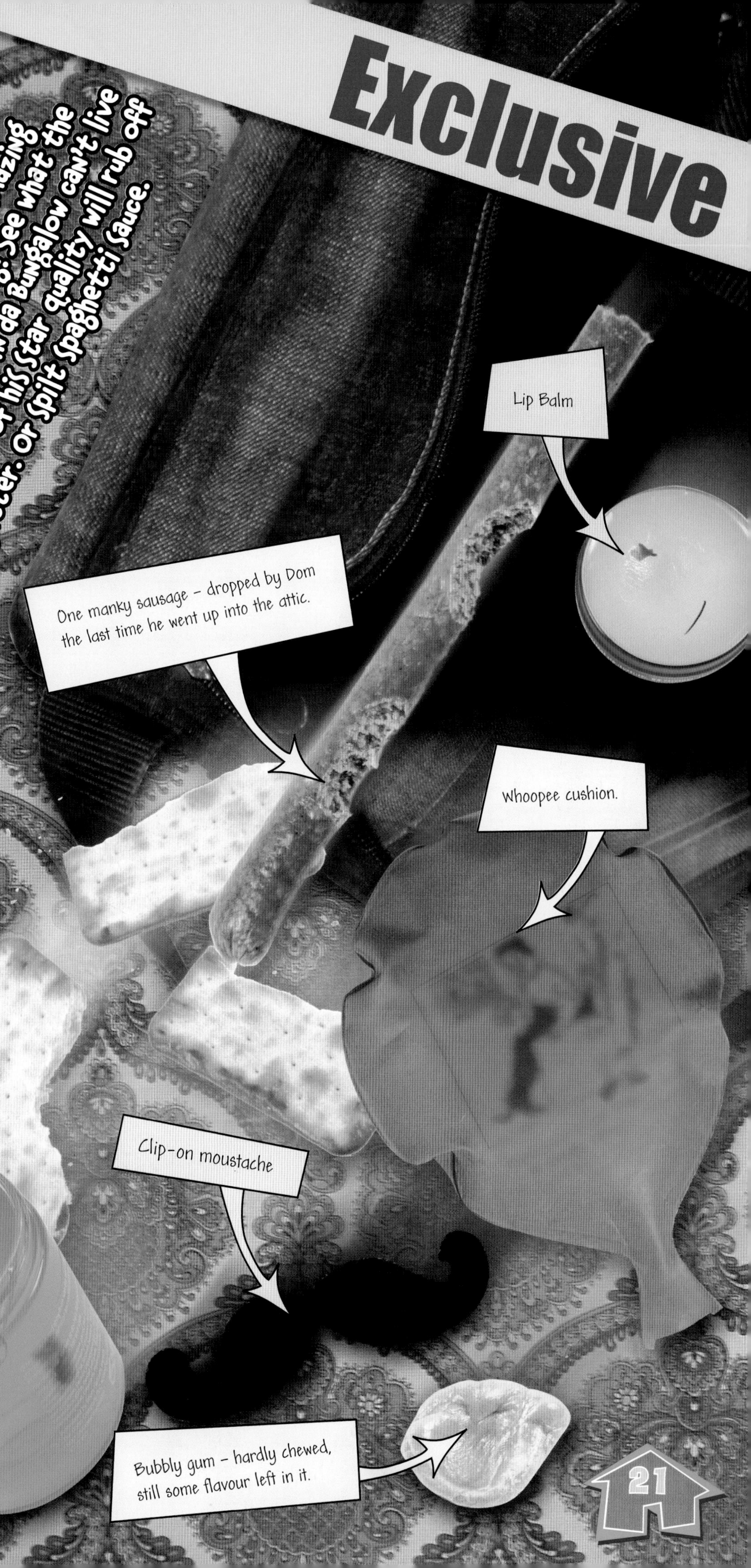

Lip Balm

One manky sausage – dropped by Dom the last time he went up into the attic.

Whoopee cushion.

Cream cracker.

Hair gel

Clip-on moustache

Bubbly gum – hardly chewed, still some flavour left in it.

Dick & Dom's SCHOOL DAZE

You! yes, you at the back! Do you think Something's funny? Do you want to come up here and Share it with the rest of the class? yes, you do? And it's Dick and Dom's School Survival guide. Oh, alright then – go ahead!

DICK'S TOP TEN HOMEWORK EXCUSES

- I didn't do it because I didn't want to make Dom look bad.
- My baby brother was sick on it.
- A big bully dared to suggest that you were not the best teacher in the school and my homework got torn up in the fight as I defended your name.
- Aliens who wanted to study the workings of a perfect human brain took it away.
- I saw a gnome stranded on a lily pad and I had to fashion a small boat out of my homework so I could rescue it. You'll be relieved to know that no harm came to the gnome, but my homework was wrecked.
- We ran out of fuel for the stove and my Dad burned my homework.
- We ran out of bread and my Dad toasted my homework.
- Our newspaper didn't arrive this morning and my Dad took my homework to read on the train.
- I ran out of undercrackers and had to use my homework to make some paper pants. I can still hand it in though, if you like.
- What homework?

DOM'S TOP TEN EXCUSES FOR BEING LATE

- I'VE NEVER BEEN TO SCHOOL ON TIME SO I WASN'T SURE WHEN IT STARTED.
- YES, I AM LATE, BUT IF THIS WERE NEW YORK THEN I'D BE WAY, WAY EARLY.
- IT'S REALLY WINDY, AND I'M ONLY SMALL SO I GOT BLOWN INTO A TREE AND THEN I HAD TO SIT ON A LEAF AND WAIT UNTIL AUTUMN SO I COULD GET DOWN.
- IF I WAS A BIT LATER, I COULD HAVE COME UP WITH A BETTER EXCUSE.
- I ASKED MY DAD FOR AN ENCYCLOPAEDIA BUT HE TOLD ME I HAD TO WALK TO SCHOOL LIKE EVERYBODY ELSE.
- WE RAN OUT OF FUEL FOR THE STOVE AND MY DAD BURNED MY WATCH.
- WE RAN OUT OF BREAD AND MY DAD TOASTED MY WATCH.
- OUR NEWSPAPER DIDN'T ARRIVE THIS MORNING AND MY DAD TOOK MY WATCH TO READ ON THE TRAIN.
- I RAN OUT OF UNDERCRACKERS AND HAD TO USE MY WATCH TO MAKE SOME PANTS. THE WATCH STILL WORKS BUT IT'S MUCH MORE DIFFICULT TO CHECK THE TIME.
- I'M LATE? I THOUGHT YOU WERE EARLY.

Dear Mr Jim Apparatus
Please excuse Richard from games today. He has a weak chimr-chimmer knee and his doctor has recommended that he keep it rested at all times

He also has a twisted cheroo. Eating chocolate helps, apparently.

Yours sincerely
Mrs McCourt

Dear Mrs McCourt,

Your son, Richard, has been caught copying answers from his friend Dominic.

Question 21 in a recent Geography test asked, “What is the capital of Australia?”

Dominic answered the question, “I don’t know.”

Richard answered, “Neither do I.”

Perhaps you can understand now why we felt it necessary to separate Richard and Dominic in Geography class.

Kind regards,

Mr. Atlas

Dear Mrs Wood,

I have reason to believe that your son, Dominic, and his friend Richard McCourt have been cheating in their exams.

Question 12 on the English paper asked, “What have you learned from reading the book ‘The Life of Florence Nightingale’?”

Richard answered the question, “She dies at the end.”

Dominic wrote exactly the same answer.

I hope you understand now why it was that Dominic and Richard were made to write out a thousand times, “I must not mindlessly copy something out.”

Kind regards,

Mrs. Oxymoron

~~School~~ Uniformly Uncomfortable

You can't leave the house looking like that! Except you can, because it's your icky school uniform – starchy collars, sensible shoes and scratchy knitwear. Who's idea was that? Come on – loosen that tie, pop your collar and let's try and get a little more comfortable.

Boys. If you're looking the way you like and liking the way you look, then you're not wearing the correct uniform. The simple rule of school uniforms is: anything that's comfortable, or looks cool, is not allowed.

Girls. Before you leave the house, ask yourself – does that tie go with that blazer? Would your Mum and Dad approve of what you're wearing? And does it make you feel uncomfortable? If the answers are "Yes", "Oh, yes", and "Most definitely and emphatically YES!" then you're wearing school uniform. Well done.

Dom's teacher once told him his shirt wasn't tucked in properly and that he should do something about it. So he took off his trousers.

Remember – there's more than one way to tie a tie! They're not just for necks, you know! Try wearing your tie around your head, around your wrist or even on your bag! This display of individuality and ingenuity will guarantee you're popular with all your teachers.

Remember to wear your blazer every day – if you remember to wear a shirt as well, that helps.

If anyone ever tells you that you have your shoes on the wrong feet then just tell them, "But these are the only feet I have!"

Right. Now you're looking totally square, it's time to get down to some serious mucking about. And the first lesson is...

HUMAN BIOLOGY

Ah, the wonders of the human body! Explore them here with this fascinating cutaway, and then astound everyone with your newfangled knowledge!

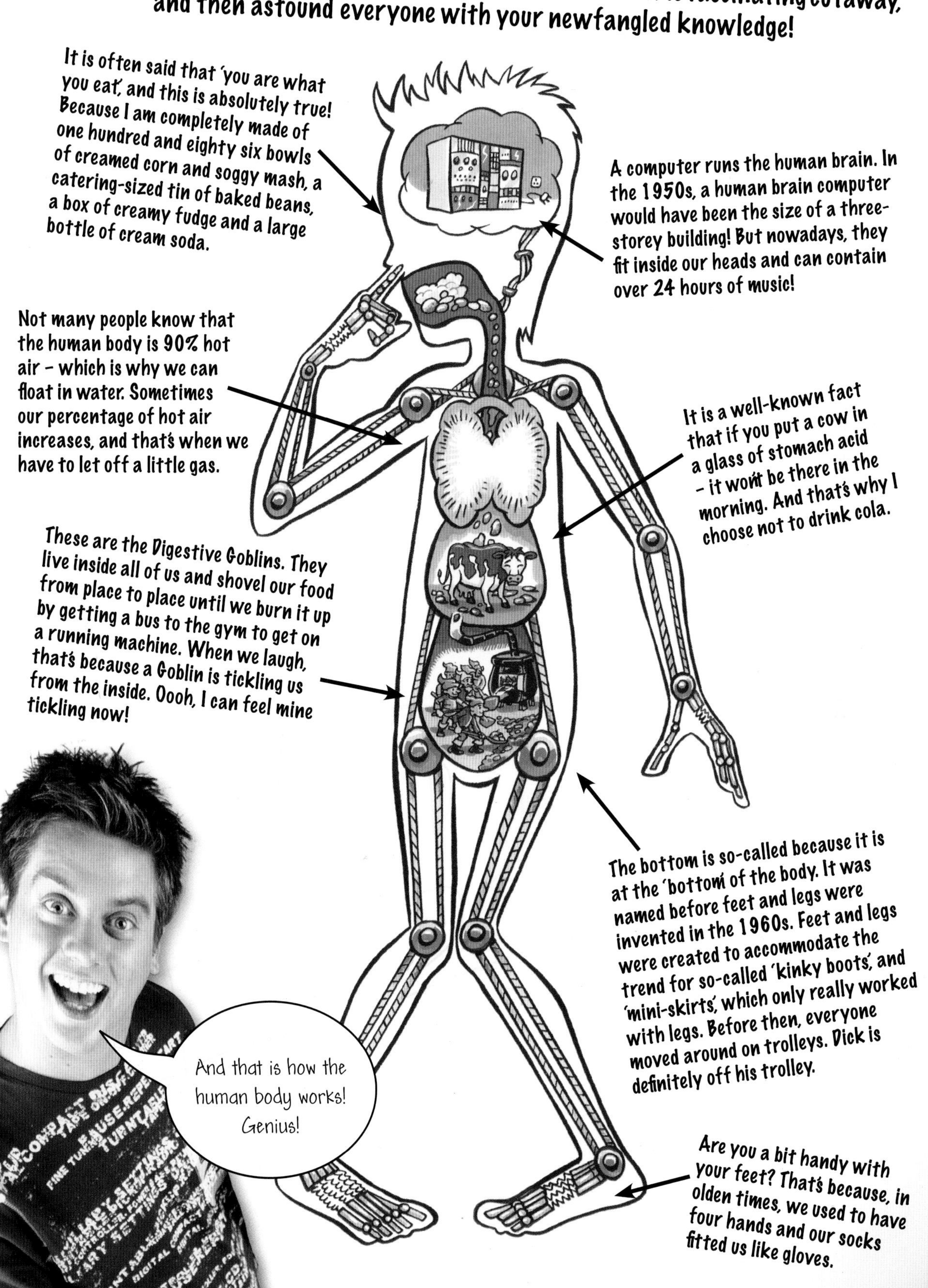

It is often said that 'you are what you eat', and this is absolutely true! Because I am completely made of one hundred and eighty six bowls of creamed corn and soggy mash, a catering-sized tin of baked beans, a box of creamy fudge and a large bottle of cream soda.
A computer runs the human brain. In the 1950s, a human brain computer would have been the size of a three-storey building! But nowadays, they fit inside our heads and can contain over 24 hours of music!
Not many people know that the human body is 90% hot air – which is why we can float in water. Sometimes our percentage of hot air increases, and that's when we have to let off a little gas.
It is a well-known fact that if you put a cow in a glass of stomach acid – it won't be there in the morning. And that's why I choose not to drink cola.
These are the Digestive Goblins. They live inside all of us and shovel our food from place to place until we burn it up by getting a bus to the gym to get on a running machine. When we laugh, that's because a Goblin is tickling us from the inside. Oooh, I can feel mine tickling now!
The bottom is so-called because it is at the 'bottom' of the body. It was named before feet and legs were invented in the 1960s. Feet and legs were created to accommodate the trend for so-called 'kinky boots' and 'mini-skirts', which only really worked with legs. Before then, everyone moved around on trolleys. Dick is definitely off his trolley.
Are you a bit handy with your feet? That's because, in olden times, we used to have four hands and our socks fitted us like gloves.
And that is how the human body works! Genius!

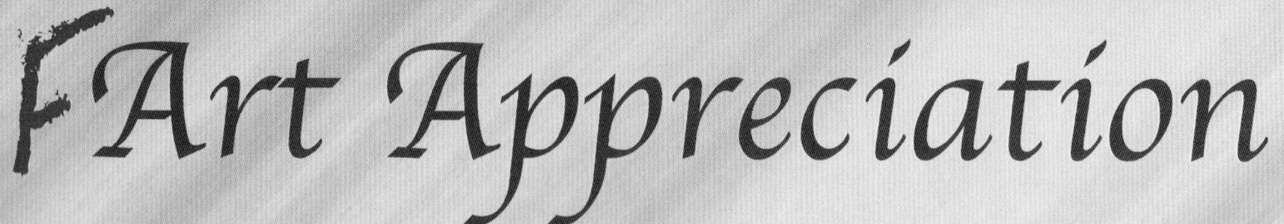

FArt Appreciation

Wow, I like this one!

Movement Number 2 – Juan Pollock, 1943

Yes, it reminds me of the carpet after a busy Saturday morning at da Bungalow.

This one's cool! It's so small and round and, wait a minute...yes! Minty!

Ah! That's where I left my half-sucked sweetie!

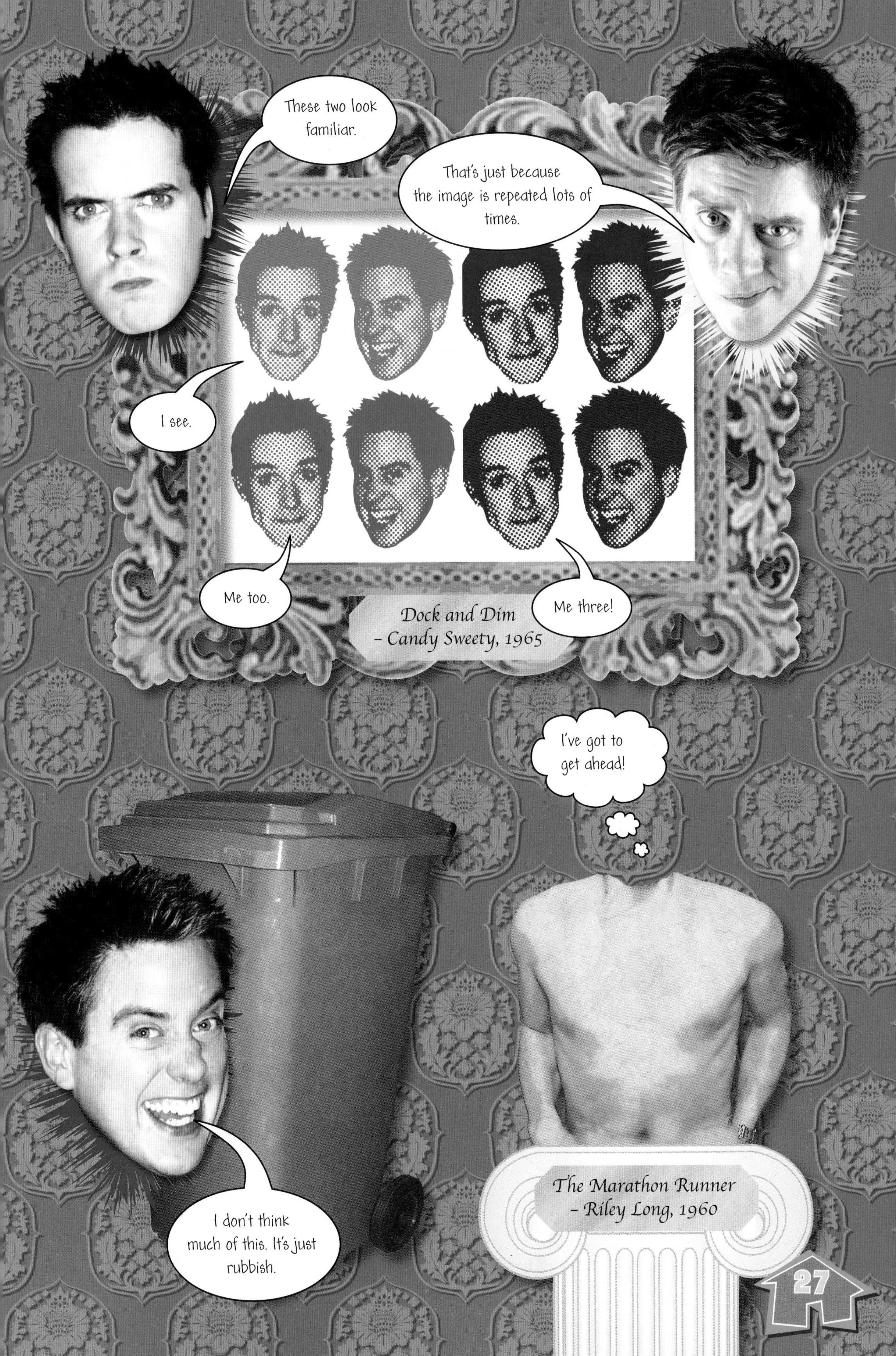

Dock and Dim
– Candy Sweety, 1965

The Marathon Runner
– Riley Long, 1960

Bogies!

Dick and Dom's really important

HISTORY

of ye whole olde worlde

You can't know where you are going without knowing where you've come from, right – especially if you're walking backwards through a hall of mirrors. Or something. Whatever, history is a mad important subject so listen up to our history lesson and pay total attention to the amazing timeline we have created for your better learning!

1 Million B.C. – Prehistoric thingy. These things just floated around a lot. Floating, floating, floating... Not that interesting really, let's fast forward a bit...

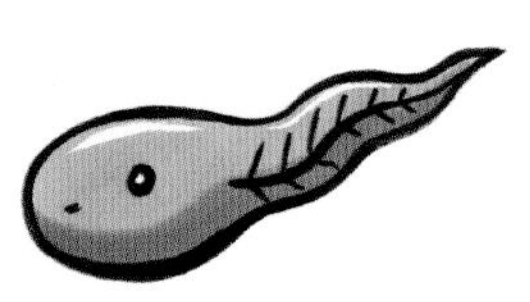

148,000 B.C. – Neanderthal man. Way back in time there was history. And so much of it. That's when this chap was around. Neanderthal man – or Cave Dom to his mates – was smaller, less intelligent and more rugged than most people nowadays. He was probably really smelly because soap hadn't been invented and they didn't have supermarkets and so he must have experimented with different kinds of food – eating and sometimes getting sick and making a mess and stuff. We've come a long, long way since then!

400 B.C. – Archimedes shouted, "Eureka!" And his wife said, "And you don't smell too fresh yourself!"

100 B.C. – Gravy was invented but as a weapon to slip up giants, rather than a tasty accompaniment to runny mash.

500 A.D. – Roman Times. These were topsy-turvy times – people wore sheets instead of clothes, covered their beds in jackets and trousers and slept upside down like vampire bats.

501 A.D. – King Arthur and stuff. There were loads of knights and horses and magic and stuff around at this time, as well as elves and gnomes and Hobbits crossing the land in search of adventure. Everyone drank mead from cups made of horns and then rolled around in the muck outside for a lark.

1 Million B.C.	148,000 B.C.	400 B.C.	100 B.C.	500 A.D.	501 A.D.	800 A.D.

Adz woz ere

800 A.D. - The Dark Ages. Not much is known about the dark ages because it was really...dark. It was so dark that no one could tell if they were asleep or awake unless they were flying and then they were asleep because no one had invented flying yet so they must have been dreaming. It was so dark, even shadows had shadows. So dark, in fact, that you could see better with your eyes shut. Did I mention it was dark?

900 A.D. - Middle Ages. Around this time, everyone was Middle Aged. Even little kids wore slippers, went to bed early and moaned a lot about people "hanging about on street corners."

1815 A.D. - The Battle of Waterloo was fought using rather disgusting weapons.

1926 A.D. - John Logie-Baird sent the first television images of himself, throwing Creamy Muck Muck over some kids.

1965 A.D. - Hippies. The Hippies were peace-loving people with big hair. They tried to change the world by wearing big flappy collars, swinging their pants and growing their beards (women too). Cool, man.

2001 A.D. - A monolith appears on Earth's moon and sends out a signal to Jupiter.

1790 A.D. - The Romantics. Romanticism was an intellectual movement - that's like when you think about going somewhere and doing something, but you don't, you just think about it. The Romantics listened to loads of bands like The Human League and Duran Duran, they wore tonnes of eyeliner and used lots and lots of hairspray until there was a hole in the ozone layer.

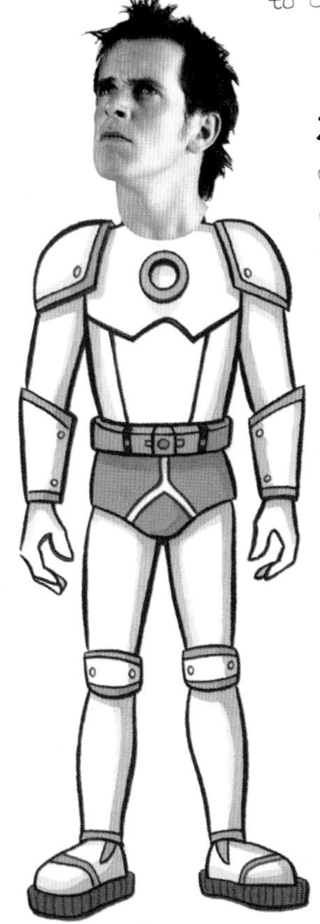

2005 A.D. - Now! Here we are today and the world is just as predicted in such prophetic texts as Buck Rogers in the 21st Century and Space: 1999! Everyone wears white unitards and lilac shakywigs and travels about on monorails. Not that we need to travel anywhere as we have everything we need in our own bubble homes! No one eats anything except special protein pills and there's no need for toilets as we all merely exude just a little dry powder.

900 A.D. | **1790 A.D.** | **1815 A.D.** | **1926 A.D.** | **1965 A.D.** | **2001 A.D.** | **2005 A.D.**

I don't eat my friends! I ♥ Dom

DOMESTIC SCIENCE

Try cooking up these grim-looking treats next time you have a Dick and Dom-style sleepover!

Pizz-urrrgh!

Have fun with this but remember – you've GOT to eat it! So you can use anything you like – as long as you like it!

Ingredients:

- **Margarita pizza**
- **Toppings of your choice**

1 Remove all the packaging from your margarita pizza and heat the oven as per the instructions on the packet.

2 Prepare the toppings of your choice. You could use pineapple chunks and marshmallows. Or think about unexpected combinations like olives and baked beans. You can use whatever you like – it's your pizz-urgh!

3 Cook the pizza as per the instructions – that's usually for about ten minutes, but keep an eye on the oven to see what happens to your crazy toppings!

Enjoy!

Dirty Norris

This gloopy brown slop is actually rather delicious!

Ingredients:

- **1 cup crunchy peanut butter**
- **1 cup plain yoghurt**
- **2 tablespoons chopped spring or salad onions or shallots**
- **1 tablespoon nut oil**
- **1-2 tablespoons soy sauce**
- **Raw veggie sticks for serving**

1 Stir together the peanut butter and yoghurt.

2 Add the rest of the ingredients (except the veggie sticks) and mix well.

3 Serve the 'Dirty Norris,' with sticks of raw carrot, celery, sweet pepper or cucumber and dig in!

Bogey Jelly

This is a great gross-out treat for a party.

Ingredients:

- **1 packet lime jelly**
- **1 packet jelly sweets or fruit gums**

1. Prepare the jelly mixture as per the instructions on the packet.
2. While the jelly mixture is cooling, sort out the sweets. Take out all the lime and lemon flavour jellies or gums and put the rest to one side.
3. Drop the lime and lemon flavour sweets into the jelly mixture, just before you put the lime jelly into the fridge.
4. When the jelly is set, it will be wobbly but full of chewy 'bogies'!

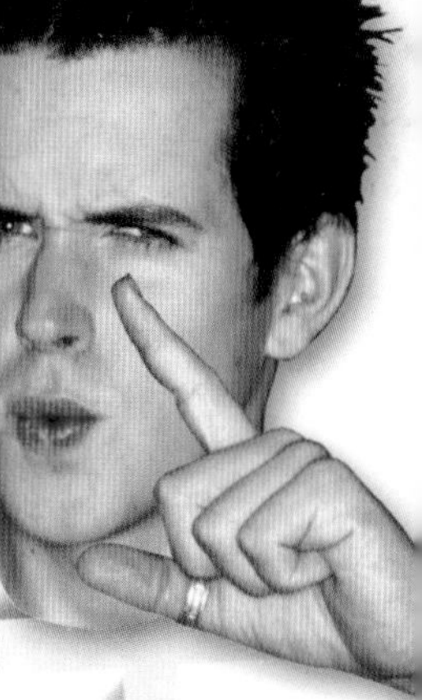

Don't forget – even we get a grown-up to help us in the kitchen!

Big Fat Maggots

Nanny Nob Nob loves these maggoty treats and eats them all the time – that's why all her teeth have fallen out.

Ingredients:

- **250g desiccated coconut**
- **200g sweetened condensed milk**
- **1 teaspoon vanilla essence**
- **A little butter or margarine**

1. Preheat the oven to 180°C/350F/gas mark 4.
2. Grease an oven tray with a little butter or margarine, or line with greaseproof paper
3. Mix all the ingredients together in a bowl.
4. Drop a teaspoon at a time onto the baking tray and mould the dollop into a maggot shape. Leave a little space between each maggot.
5. If you want, you can finely chop some glace cherries and add 'eyes'.
6. Bake for ten minutes or until your maggots are lightly browned.
7. Remove from baking tray and leave to cool on a wire rack.

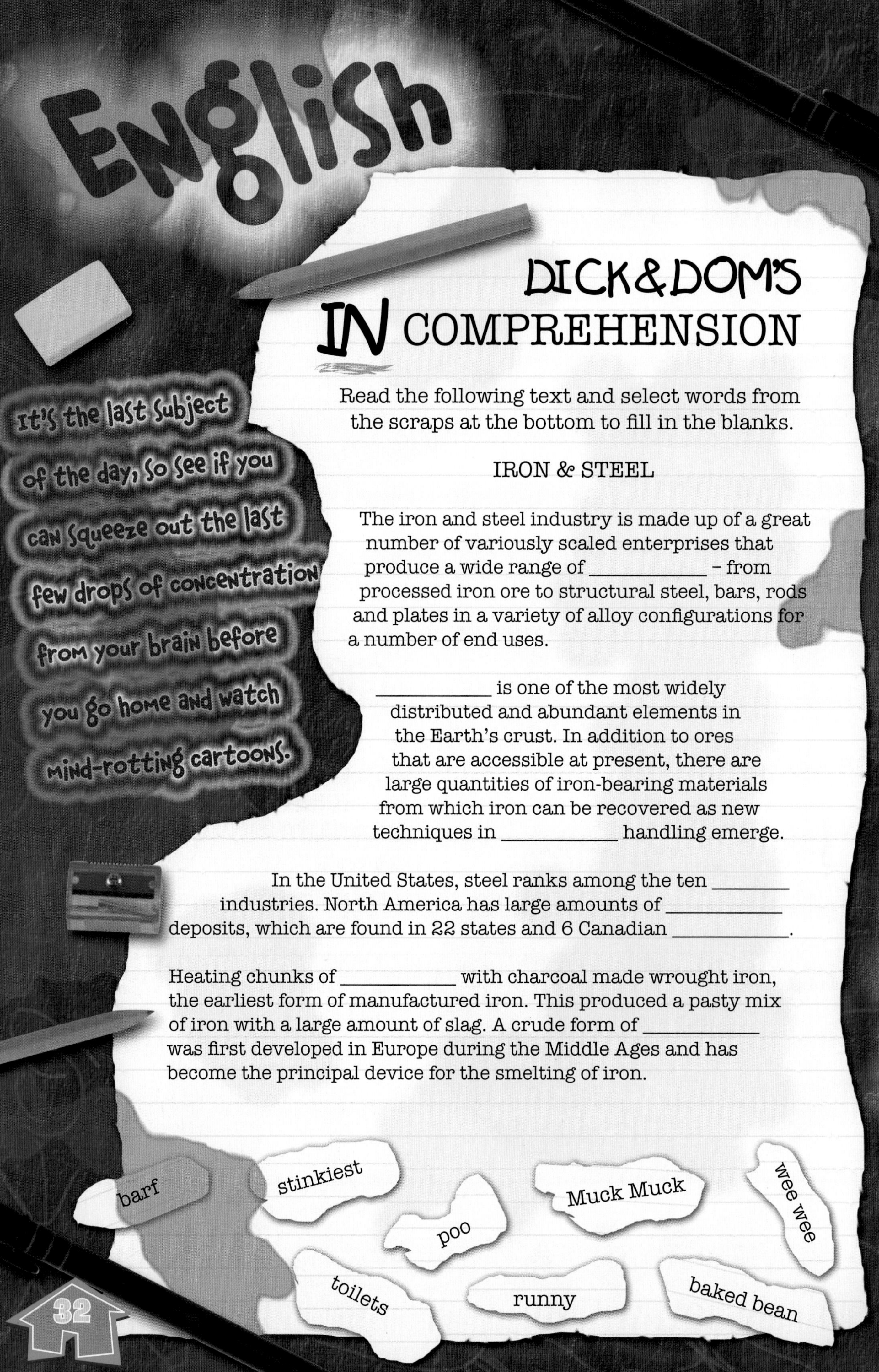

English

DICK & DOM'S IN COMPREHENSION

It's the last subject of the day, so see if you can squeeze out the last few drops of concentration from your brain before you go home and watch mind-rotting cartoons.

Read the following text and select words from the scraps at the bottom to fill in the blanks.

IRON & STEEL

The iron and steel industry is made up of a great number of variously scaled enterprises that produce a wide range of ___________ – from processed iron ore to structural steel, bars, rods and plates in a variety of alloy configurations for a number of end uses.

___________ is one of the most widely distributed and abundant elements in the Earth's crust. In addition to ores that are accessible at present, there are large quantities of iron-bearing materials from which iron can be recovered as new techniques in ___________ handling emerge.

In the United States, steel ranks among the ten _______ industries. North America has large amounts of ___________ deposits, which are found in 22 states and 6 Canadian ___________.

Heating chunks of ___________ with charcoal made wrought iron, the earliest form of manufactured iron. This produced a pasty mix of iron with a large amount of slag. A crude form of ___________ was first developed in Europe during the Middle Ages and has become the principal device for the smelting of iron.

barf

stinkiest

poo

Muck Muck

wee wee

toilets

runny

baked bean

Ah! Poetry! Not just a metrical and rhymed composition, but also an art form associated with highly refined language and in possession of the sort of sensuous and rhythmic qualities that seem to satisfy a fundamental human need! Let us celebrate poetry on this page! Let us revel in it the same way a golden retriever puppy might roll around in a fresh cowpat in a summer meadow. Read on, dear reader – read on!

As I sat under the apple tree,
A birdie sent his love to me,
And as I wiped it from my eye,
I said, "Thank goodness cows can't fly!"

1819, little Alfred Tennyson, age 10

Ip dip doo, doggy did a poo,
Cat does a wee wee, out goes you.

1779, William Wordsworth, age 9

The peanut sat on the railway track; his heart was all aflutter,
Along came a train, the nine fifteen, toot toot – peanut butter.

1570, Will Shakespeare, age 6

Eeny, meeny, miney, mo
Put the baby on the po,
when it's done, wipe its bum,
Eeny, meeny, miney mum.

1848, Thomas Hardy, age 8

Mrs white, had a fright, in the middle of the night,
Saw a ghost, eating toast, halfway up a lamppost.

1938, Ted Hughes (after Ben Jonson), age 8

Mary had a little lamb; she also had a bear,
I've often seen her little lamb, but never seen her bear.

1932, DH Lawrence, age 47

Ring the bell! School's out! That's the end of the brainiac section – let's hope you've learned something!

DICK AND DOM'S PLEASANT WAYS TO PASS THE TIME.

Ah, autumn – season of mists and mellow fruitfulness. But what about the other three seasons? Don't let a whole year pass like nothing – do something meaningful with your time! That's right, we're talking about pastimes! Take up a hobby, start a collection or join in with a sport! You might be dazzled by all these choices so it's lucky for you that we're on hand to help!

Karaoke

Everyone loves to get up and sing – even if they pretend they don't. What's especially good is changing some of the words. Here's a list of our ten favourite words to insert randomly into song lyrics:

Wig
Loo
Bot
Toot
Cheese sandwich
Poopy woo
Splatty log
Lumpy trump
Bibble
Verisimilitude

STAMP COLLECTING

Don't be put off by the spoddy image of stamp collecting. Looking at pictures of, say, racing cars on stamps can be just as exciting as getting into a real racing car and winning a race! Putting your stamps in an album is the most exciting part of stamp collecting – and saves all of the hassle of having to send or receive a letter with a stamp on it.

BOGEY BOARDING

Bogey boarding sounds like a thrilling 'extreme' sport, but it's actually simply the art of collecting bogies on a board. While speeding down a snowy mountain.

Tiddlywinks

Tiddlywinks is an actual sport and getting the right protective gear can be prohibitively expensive. But, worry not, because you can improvise. Tying cushions around your chest using your dressing gown belt can create body armour. Cereal packets make excellent clogs and – once you slip your feet into a couple of empty cornflake packets you'll never fear an accidentally dropped tiddlywink again!

FLOWER PRESSING

Most people think that pressing flowers means having to pick them. Not true. We respect our flower friends! To us, 'pressing flowers,' means taking a good long walk and pressing a few flowers – you can do this outdoors, but if you've got house plants then indoors can be almost as rewarding. To press a flower, hold it carefully between your thumb and a finger (your index – or pointing – finger is best but any of the others will do) and press it – gently now! Then simply move on, knowing Mother Nature is smiling down on you...or up at you. She's all around, remember, and always watching! So behave...and keep the Country Code!

Colin's Dictionary

A

Aboard: a special device for getting onto a boat
Austere: what I do with the handlebars of my bike
Autobahn: a German garage
Autobiography: the logbook of a car

B

Bison: where to wash your face in North America
Brouhaha: French word for tea (they drink coffee in France, they think tea is funny.)

C

Chateau: French small talk
Chopstick: an axe

D

Denial: the longest river in the world…er, that isn't the Amazon
Doggerel: the language dogs speak

E

Eclipse: what a barber does
Extinct: the stale smell of old jokes

F

Fiasco: Italian action painting
Fjord: Norwegian car

G

Gladiator: how a cannibal feels after a good meal

H

Humbug: a bee

I

Ice lolly: frozen assets

J

Jigsaw: what you get if you dance in tight pants

K

Ketchup: the last sauce to run out
Kidnap: Dom's afternoon rest

L

Largo: Italian beer
Libretto: Italian open-toed sandal

M

Maritime: the wedding season

N

Nightmare: a dark horse

O

Octopus: a cat with eight legs

O

Ooze: a river that creeps through York city centre at 11pm on a Friday night
Optimist: a special kind of doctor who looks right into your eyes and tells you that you're really well

P

Pheasants: French peasants
Phillipe Phillip: French inventor of beachwear
Polygon: an empty birdcage
Pot-pourri: French toilet

Q

Queue: a line of snooker players

R

Relief: the feeling you get when you look at trees in spring
Refined: located lost sugar

S

Sewage: a canal in Egypt
Surname: what you call your male teachers

T

Telepathy: a sixth sense belonging to people who instinctively know when it's time for their favourite TV show
Troubadour: Where you go when you step outside

U

Udder: a snake that produces milk
Underlay: South American carpet insulation
Union: where to attach your kneepads

V

Verbal contract: not worth the paper it's written on

W

Walkie-talkie: someone who is usually so daft, you're amazed when they can do two things at once e.g. The Prize Idiot
Weight: the heavy feeling you get when you're hungry and your tea isn't ready

X

Xerox: cattle that copy your homework

Y

Yak: cattle talk
Yellow: a loud colour

Z

Zero: a dream in which you put your pants over your trousers and leap into action to save the day
Zoom: a place where fast animals are kept

ASK DR DOM

Life can be tough. And when life is tough, that's when you need tough love. Thank goodness Doctor Dom is on hand to dole it out. You can always trust Doctor Dom to tell it like it is – unless he can't and then he'll just make something up.

Dear Dr Dom,
I have a teacher who asks the class a question, and then only ever picks you if you don't put your hand up to answer. What should I do?
Love,
Hans Down

DEAR HANS, TRY PUTTING YOUR HAND UP WHEN YOU DON'T KNOW THE ANSWER. IT'S A LONG SHOT, BUT IT MIGHT JUST WORK!

Dear Doctor Dom,
As if it wasn't bad enough that I have to do a project for school, my science teacher is making me work with a boy that really smells. What should I do?
Yours,
Brian O'Pugh

DEAR BO, SUGGEST TO YOUR STINKY CLASSMATE THAT YOU DO THE WHOLE PROJECT OVER THE PHONE.

Dear Dr Dom,
We are struggling to bridge the generation gap between our son and us. He's always throwing food around and causing havoc. He thinks it's funny to shout "bogies," and he's always going on about "Dirty Norris," and "runny mash." We just don't get it. Help!
Yours sincerely,
Mr and Mrs Wood.

DEAR MR AND MRS WOOD, TRY TUNING INTO THE CBBC CHANNEL ON WEEKEND MORNINGS. THERE ARE TWO LADS ON THERE THAT GET THEMSELVES INTO A RIGHT OLD MESS. PAY CLOSE ATTENTION AND YOU'LL SOON SEE WHAT IT'S ALL ABOUT!

Dear Dr Dom,
By the time I've completed my daily ablutions, I never seem to have enough time for breakfast in the morning. What should I do?
Yours hurriedly,
Justin Time
P.S. If you had an extra "o" in your name, you would be a baddie in the Fantastic Four.

DEAR JUSTIN, EAT YOUR BREAKFAST BEFORE YOU GO TO BED.
P.S. SOMEDAY, THE WHOLE WORLD WILL BE MINE! HA HA HA HA!

Dear Dr Dom,
When I leave the bathroom at night, my Mum always reminds me to "put the light out." So, last night, I put the light out – right out of the window – and I got into a whole heap of trouble. Why does everything have to be so complicated?
Yours crumbly,
PI

DEAR PI EVERYTHING HAS TO BE COMPLICATED OR LIFE WOULD BE LIKE PUTTING TOGETHER A ONE-PIECE JIGSAW - I.E. NO FUN AND IT WOULDN'T TAKE LONG. HOPEFULLY YOU'LL BE AROUND FOR A FEW YEARS, PI OLD PAL AND YOU'LL HAVE TIME TO WORK IT OUT OR...HEY, WAIT A MINUTE...ARE YOU A PRIVATE INVESTIGATOR? OR IS THAT THE PRIZE IDIOT? CLEAR OFF! AND TAKE THOSE CHEESE SANDWICHES WITH YOU! FOOL!

Dear Dr Dom,
I am lonely and feel that all my friends have abandoned me.
Yours truly,
Richard McCourt

DEAR DICK, HAVE YOU THOUGHT ABOUT TAKING A SHOWER AND CHANGING YOUR PANTS?

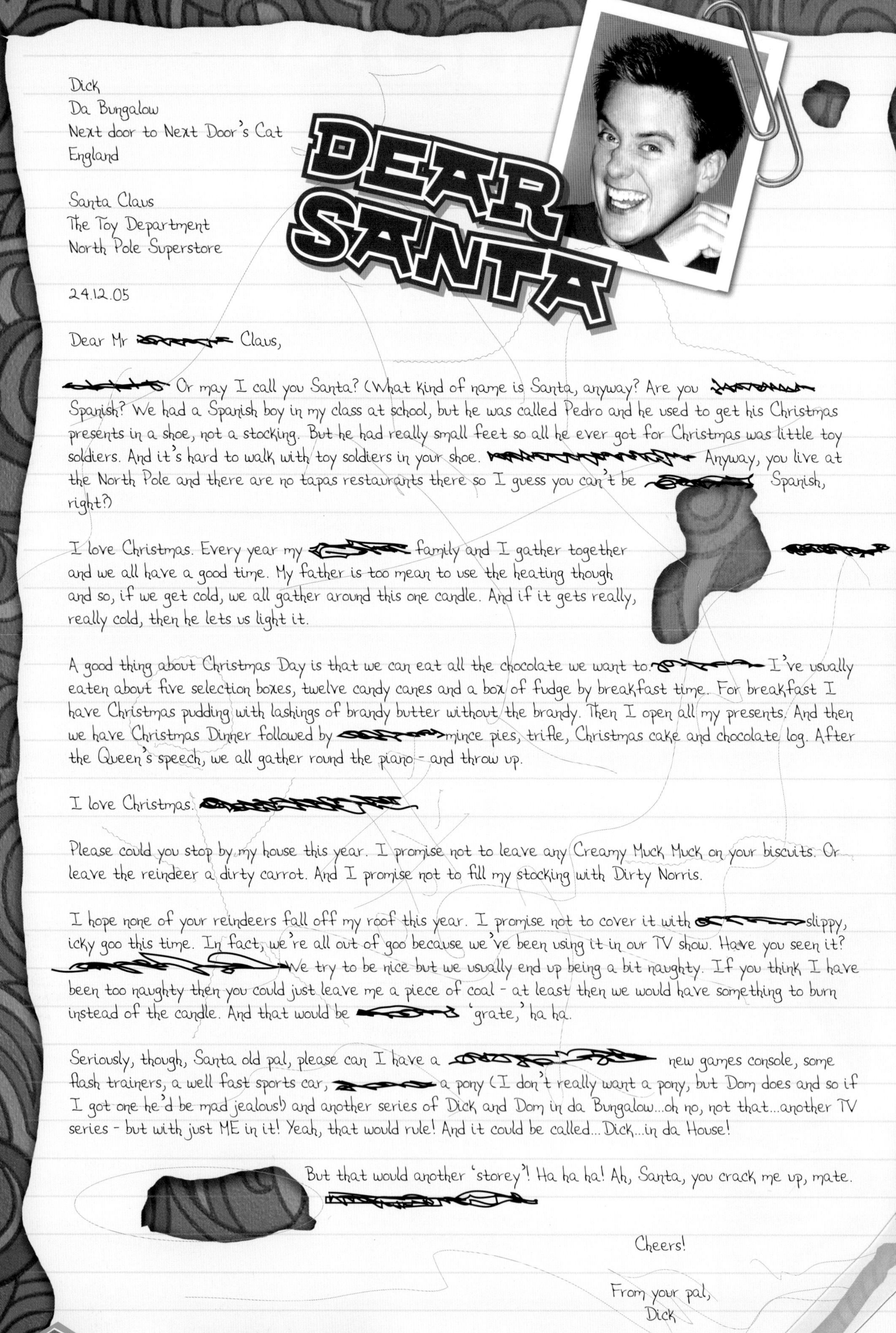

DEAR SANTA

Dick
Da Bungalow
Next door to Next Door's Cat
England

Santa Claus
The Toy Department
North Pole Superstore

24.12.05

Dear Mr Claus,

Or may I call you Santa? (What kind of name is Santa, anyway? Are you Spanish? We had a Spanish boy in my class at school, but he was called Pedro and he used to get his Christmas presents in a shoe, not a stocking. But he had really small feet so all he ever got for Christmas was little toy soldiers. And it's hard to walk with toy soldiers in your shoe. Anyway, you live at the North Pole and there are no tapas restaurants there so I guess you can't be Spanish, right?)

I love Christmas. Every year my family and I gather together and we all have a good time. My father is too mean to use the heating though and so, if we get cold, we all gather around this one candle. And if it gets really, really cold, then he lets us light it.

A good thing about Christmas Day is that we can eat all the chocolate we want to. I've usually eaten about five selection boxes, twelve candy canes and a box of fudge by breakfast time. For breakfast I have Christmas pudding with lashings of brandy butter without the brandy. Then I open all my presents. And then we have Christmas Dinner followed by mince pies, trifle, Christmas cake and chocolate log. After the Queen's speech, we all gather round the piano - and throw up.

I love Christmas.

Please could you stop by my house this year. I promise not to leave any Creamy Muck Muck on your biscuits. Or leave the reindeer a dirty carrot. And I promise not to fill my stocking with Dirty Norris.

I hope none of your reindeers fall off my roof this year. I promise not to cover it with slippy, icky goo this time. In fact, we're all out of goo because we've been using it in our TV show. Have you seen it? We try to be nice but we usually end up being a bit naughty. If you think I have been too naughty then you could just leave me a piece of coal - at least then we would have something to burn instead of the candle. And that would be 'grate,' ha ha.

Seriously, though, Santa old pal, please can I have a new games console, some flash trainers, a well fast sports car, a pony (I don't really want a pony, but Dom does and so if I got one he'd be mad jealous!) and another series of Dick and Dom in da Bungalow...oh no, not that...another TV series - but with just ME in it! Yeah, that would rule! And it could be called... Dick...in da House!

But that would another 'storey'! Ha ha ha! Ah, Santa, you crack me up, mate.

Cheers!

From your pal,
Dick

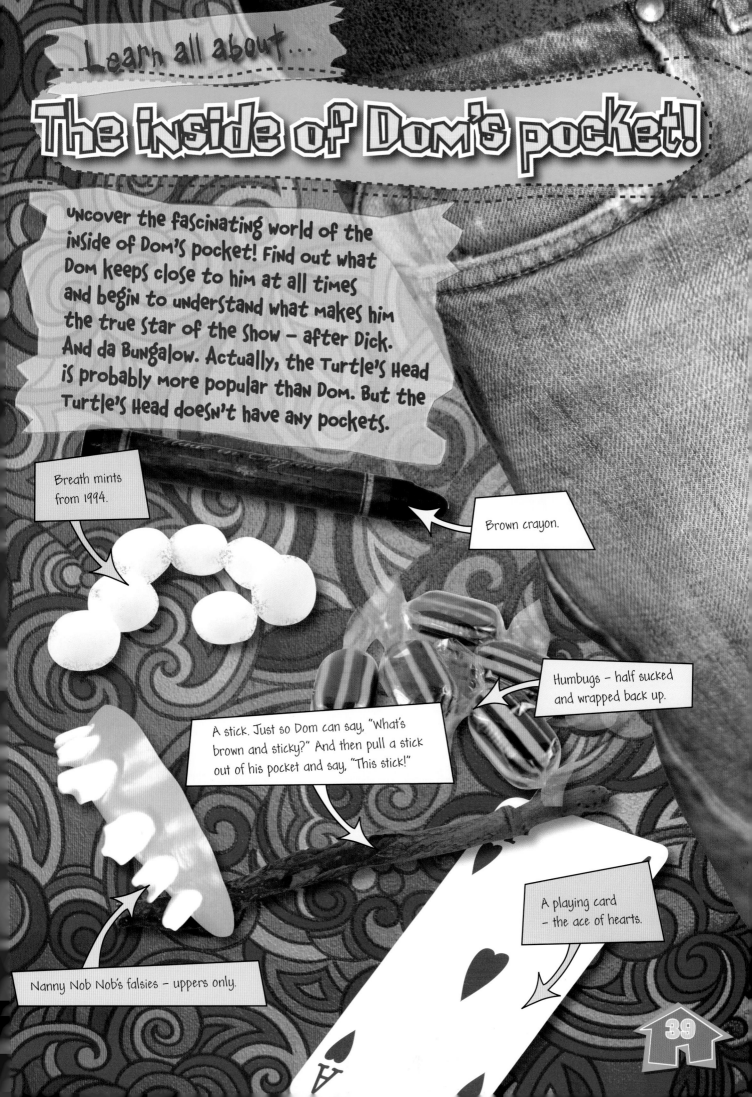

Learn all about...

The inside of Dom's pocket!

Uncover the fascinating world of the inside of Dom's pocket! Find out what Dom keeps close to him at all times and begin to understand what makes him the true star of the show – after Dick. And da Bungalow. Actually, the Turtle's Head is probably more popular than Dom. But the Turtle's Head doesn't have any pockets.

Breath mints from 1994.

Brown crayon.

Humbugs – half sucked and wrapped back up.

A stick. Just so Dom can say, "What's brown and sticky?" And then pull a stick out of his pocket and say, "This stick!"

A playing card – the ace of hearts.

Nanny Nob Nob's falsies – uppers only.

MAKE DICK SICK...

...Or make him climb a tree or do a silly dance!

Yes, it's your chance to turn the tables on Dick and Dom and get the little monkeys to do what YOU want! It's totally up to you what happens as you choose your own path through this silly story! Pick one box of each colour, to create your own story...

Start Here!

It was nine o'clock on a Saturday night and Dick was alone in da Bungalow. It was a little bit dark and a little bit scary and he was listening out for the slightest sound when...

Start

It was nine o'clock on a Saturday morning and Dick was alone in da Bungalow. He had just started to wonder where Dom was when...

Start

Once upon a time, in a place called 'da Bungalow,' little Dick Riding Hood was skipping through the forest when...

Start

It was nineteen o'clock on the twelfth of never and Dick Bibentucker was all alone in the building. He thought he could smell a rat. And he was right...

Start

A long time ago, in a Bungalow far, far away...

The phone rang – tring tring! Dick picked up the phone. It was Dom's Mum. She said...

The doorbell rang – bing bong! It was The Prize Idiot from next door, wearing his flippers and a funny hat. The Prize Idiot said...

A thought struck Dick – could he manage to spend a whole Saturday without his pal, Dom? But his train of thought was derailed when the Moose said...

Dick saw a hungry-looking wolf picking flowers. The wolf turned his big, round eyes upon Dick and said...

There was the sound of distant gunfire. Somewhere in the city, a crime was being committed. Or perhaps someone was watching an old movie in the next room. Either way, there was only one thing to say about it...

"I'm sorry to say that Dom can't come round to play today, he's at home with a cold." "Oh, dear," said Dick. "I am sorry to hear that." But then he heard a stifled giggle and Dick said...

"Dom's up a tree with a monkey. Can I do the show with you today?" And, quick as a flash, Dick said...

"BUUUURRRRP!" And Dick replied...

"Aaarrrggghhh!" And Dick jumped right up in the air. "You, idiot!" yelled Dick. "I almost dropped my sausage!" Because, oh yes, Dick was eating a sausage. So Dick ate the sausage and then he said...

"This is the end of the line. I never thought we'd make it, kid, but we have." Dick was puzzled. Where was the voice coming from? He decided to confront the intruder and said...

"I think that's Dom putting on a silly voice!" "You're right," said Dom. "It's only me. Can I come in?" And so Dom entered da Bungalow. "Thank goodness you're alright," said Dick. "For a minute there I thought you were..."

"Can I smell cabbage gravy or have you just...?" But he was interrupted as Dom swung through the window on a vine. He was wearing a monkey suit, but without the mask. Dick jumped back in surprise. "Dom!" shouted Dick, "I thought you were..."

"That was DISGUSTING! I wish Dom was here to have heard it!" And there was a laugh and the Moose said, "It's me! I'm Dom!" And Dick looked at the Moose's head and said, "YOU'RE Dom! I thought you were..."

"Is that you, Dom?" And Dom said, "Yes it was me all along!" And Dick said, "Well, hurry up! I thought you were never going to show up. In fact, I thought you were..."

"I am a Private Investigator – more colloquially known as a Private Eye. It takes many years of study at the school of life to qualify for this job, and I don't mind if you give me just a little respect." Dom apologised for not making his appearance in this story sooner. Dick said, "That's OK, pal. But I thought you were never going to turn up. I thought you were..."

"...not going to bother to show up today." "Nooo," said Dom, "I was only playing a little prank!" But Dom wasn't to have the last laugh, oh no, for at that very moment...

"...being very silly and only showing off in front of your friends. Birthday or no birthday, if you carry on behaving like that then you'll be sent upstairs to bed." Dom sulked for a bit before admitting Dick was probably right. He was just going to cut the birthday cake when...

"...up to your neck in Creamy Muck Muck!" "I am," said Dom, as the Creamy Muck Muck crept up to his chin. "Help me!" And so Dick reached out for his best pal Dom. "Hold on tight!" said Dick, "I'll get you out of this mess if it's the last thing I do!" Dick strained but the Creamy Muck Muck had a good tight hold of Dom and looked like it was going to swallow him all up. But at that moment...

"...and...er...oh, forget it!" said Dick. "I've no idea what I was going to say. Just mind that trap I set for you earlier today." But it was too late!

"...going to be kidnapped by aliens!" "I AM going to be kidnapped," shrieked Dom, grabbing Dick and throwing him to the floor. "Get down! Here comes their super-powered, deadly-accurate, specially-concentrated energy ray!"

ZZZAAAPPP! A huge beam of light crashed through the window and burned into the floor, smashing da Bungalow and everything in it, including Dick and Dom into a million, billion, trillion ka-zillion pieces! SCHTOOOM!

The End!

SPLOOSH! Dick and Dom were washed down the toilet and never, ever seen again – because that's what happens to naughty boys who don't wash their hands before dinner!

The End!

BLORP! Dom disappeared into the Creamy Muck Muck and was never seen again...! "Hurrah!" shouted the villagers, "The village is free to trade buttons with the wild monkeys once more – and it's all thanks to the Pied Piper!"

The End!

BZZZT! "Doctor McCourt to the surgery, Doctor McCourt to surgery!" That brought Dick out of his fantasy! He was the top surgeon in a big hospital. He was exhausted from 24 hours on call and he'd nodded off. The whole idea of him being the presenter of a crazy kids' TV show was just an elaborate daydream!

The End!

DING-A-LING! Dom's alarm clock woke him up. He prodded Dick. "Hey, guess what?" he said to his pal. "I've just had the strangest dream! What happened was..."

Go Back To Start!

DICK'S DIARY

What's it like being a television genius, called upon to come up with one great idea after another? Follow Dick – and his muse – for one week and begin to understand the mind that comes up with such Bungalow gold as the Baby Race.

Monday

A hard day's work trying to dream up great new games for our top-rated TV show.

Sharpened 362 pencils and chewed 363 more down to the nib.

Tidied my desk and sorted all the remaining pencils into size order.

Read some comics for research.

Filed all my comics alphabetically.

That didn't seem right so I took them all out and filed them thematically.

You wouldn't believe the fluff that had gathered behind the filing cabinet. There was a ball of hair down there the size of my own head.

And the windowsill! When did THAT last see a duster?

Cleaned the muck off from around my bedroom door handle. It's amazing how dirty those door handles get - and you don't even notice until you don't really have anything better to think about... I mean, until you have some space to sit quietly and think.

I was finally getting down to work when Dom came home from the shops with a new computer game. Dom wanted me to play the game with him but I wanted to get on with my work. We argued for ages and ages - at least three minutes. But Dom's my best mate and I don't like arguing with him so I agreed to play his new game for FIVE MINUTES ONLY.

The next thing I knew, my alarm clock went and it was morning.

We'd been playing ALL NIGHT.

And no matter what Dom says, I WON, OK?

Tuesday

Decided to have a nice quiet day in the library. Maybe I can get some work done there?

Got thrown out of the library for playing Bogies! I totally won with a 9.2 but Dom reckons he was way louder. We had a fight about it and then got thrown out of the bus shelter outside the library. Then we had a fight about whose fault it was that we got thrown out of the bus shelter and we got thrown out of the street.

There wasn't anywhere left to get thrown out of so we went home to da Bungalow and threw ourselves out. That kept us amused for about a minute and then it was time for tea.

A good cup of tea always helps me to concentrate! Yep, tea's the thing! A cup of tea and down to work!

Except the kettle whistled and Dom reckoned it makes the exact same noise as the first bit of the Cantina's Bar theme from Star Wars: A New Hope. So we had to go and get the DVD to check, and ended up watching all of the films one after the other...

...

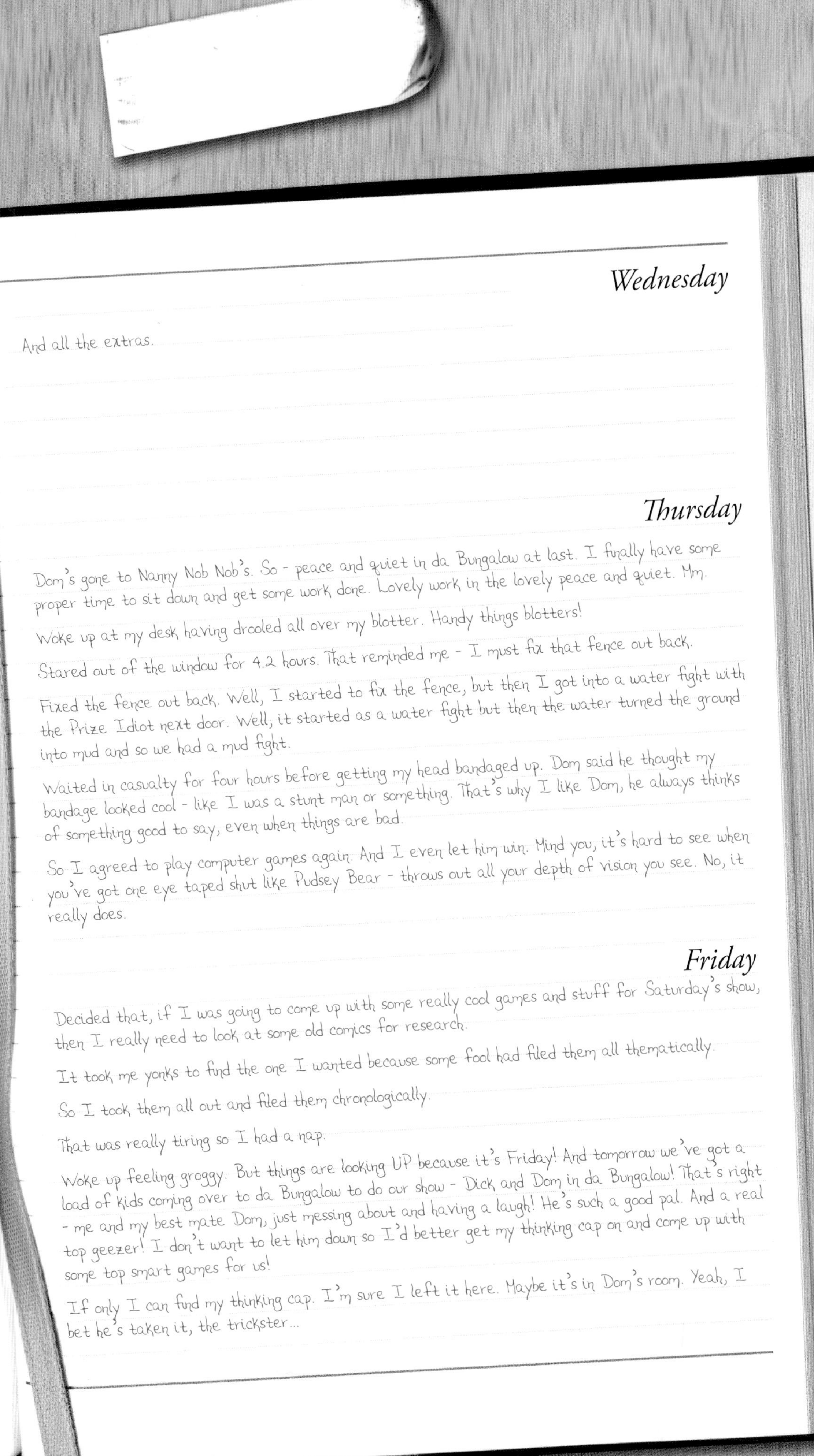

Wednesday

And all the extras.

Thursday

Dom's gone to Nanny Nob Nob's. So - peace and quiet in da Bungalow at last. I finally have some proper time to sit down and get some work done. Lovely work in the lovely peace and quiet. Mm.

Woke up at my desk having drooled all over my blotter. Handy things blotters!

Stared out of the window for 4.2 hours. That reminded me - I must fix that fence out back.

Fixed the fence out back. Well, I started to fix the fence, but then I got into a water fight with the Prize Idiot next door. Well, it started as a water fight but then the water turned the ground into mud and so we had a mud fight.

Waited in casualty for four hours before getting my head bandaged up. Dom said he thought my bandage looked cool - like I was a stunt man or something. That's why I like Dom, he always thinks of something good to say, even when things are bad.

So I agreed to play computer games again. And I even let him win. Mind you, it's hard to see when you've got one eye taped shut like Pudsey Bear - throws out all your depth of vision you see. No, it really does.

Friday

Decided that, if I was going to come up with some really cool games and stuff for Saturday's show, then I really need to look at some old comics for research.

It took me yonks to find the one I wanted because some fool had filed them all thematically.

So I took them all out and filed them chronologically.

That was really tiring so I had a nap.

Woke up feeling groggy. But things are looking UP because it's Friday! And tomorrow we've got a load of kids coming over to da Bungalow to do our show - Dick and Dom in da Bungalow! That's right - me and my best mate Dom, just messing about and having a laugh! He's such a good pal. And a real top geezer! I don't want to let him down so I'd better get my thinking cap on and come up with some top smart games for us!

If only I can find my thinking cap. I'm sure I left it here. Maybe it's in Dom's room. Yeah, I bet he's taken it, the trickster...

The Bungalow Bog

JANUARY | FULL OF FICTITIOUS RUBBISH | VOLUME NO. 010 4623

THE DOM STORY

What do we know about Dominic Wood? All together – not much. Let's look a little closer... But not too close.

On the 4th of Octember 1998, Dominic Dallas Farthing Wood, was born to Robin and Maid Marian in a grey tenement block – one of hundreds of similar buildings on the wrong side of the tracks in the windy city of Muckago. Dom always hated the stairs in those grim tenements and has lived in bungalows ever since.

Prohibition-era Muckago was a bleak place. But out of bleakness came forth sweetness – in the form of jazz music. And it was this very same music that was to provide the template for Dom's early years.

Dom was a stellar keyboardist and child prodigy. Learning to play from watching his uncle (Minty McFresh of Minty McFresh and the Fab Fresh Four) it took Dom a little while to find his feet – before he remembered he'd left them under his bed in a shoebox with his Action Man.

Dom's keyboard skills were helped by the extra fingers he'd grown in a jam jar on the windowsill of that Muckago tenement block. And, by the age of four, Dom was playing with the Muckago Symphony Orchestra.

By the age of ten, Dom – then known as 'Little Dominic Wood' – had already cut such seminal discs as *Green Muck* and *Bring Down the Norris*. Muckago was rocked by the crazy stylings of this lil' kid from uptown, downtown, in my lady's chamber.

At the age of twelve, Dom broke out of the jazz underground and went mainstream, having a worldwide crossover hit with a piece of electronic fusion called *Muckit*. Dom – now known simply as 'Dom' – had an eye for a good sound and really smelt the moment.

The sun was rising over a whole new jazzy skyline and jazz was discovering a fresh audience in the b-boys and breakers of New Muck City. Taping pieces of lino to the trolley cars that sped up and down the city's steep streets, those crazy kids popped and locked to Dom's fresh new sound. Fuelled by blanket bedtime radio play and a body-rockin' video – *Muckit* became, literally, the song that ate the world...and burped it back up again.

Following this early success, most people would have retired and gone to live on Bungalow Island. But Dom didn't rest on his laurels – he used them to make a fine wreath for his front door.

Dom describes da Bungalow as "a shaft of improvisational light in an otherwise jazz-free existence. Being popular means nothing to me now. If my work makes just one child smile then that's enough for me."

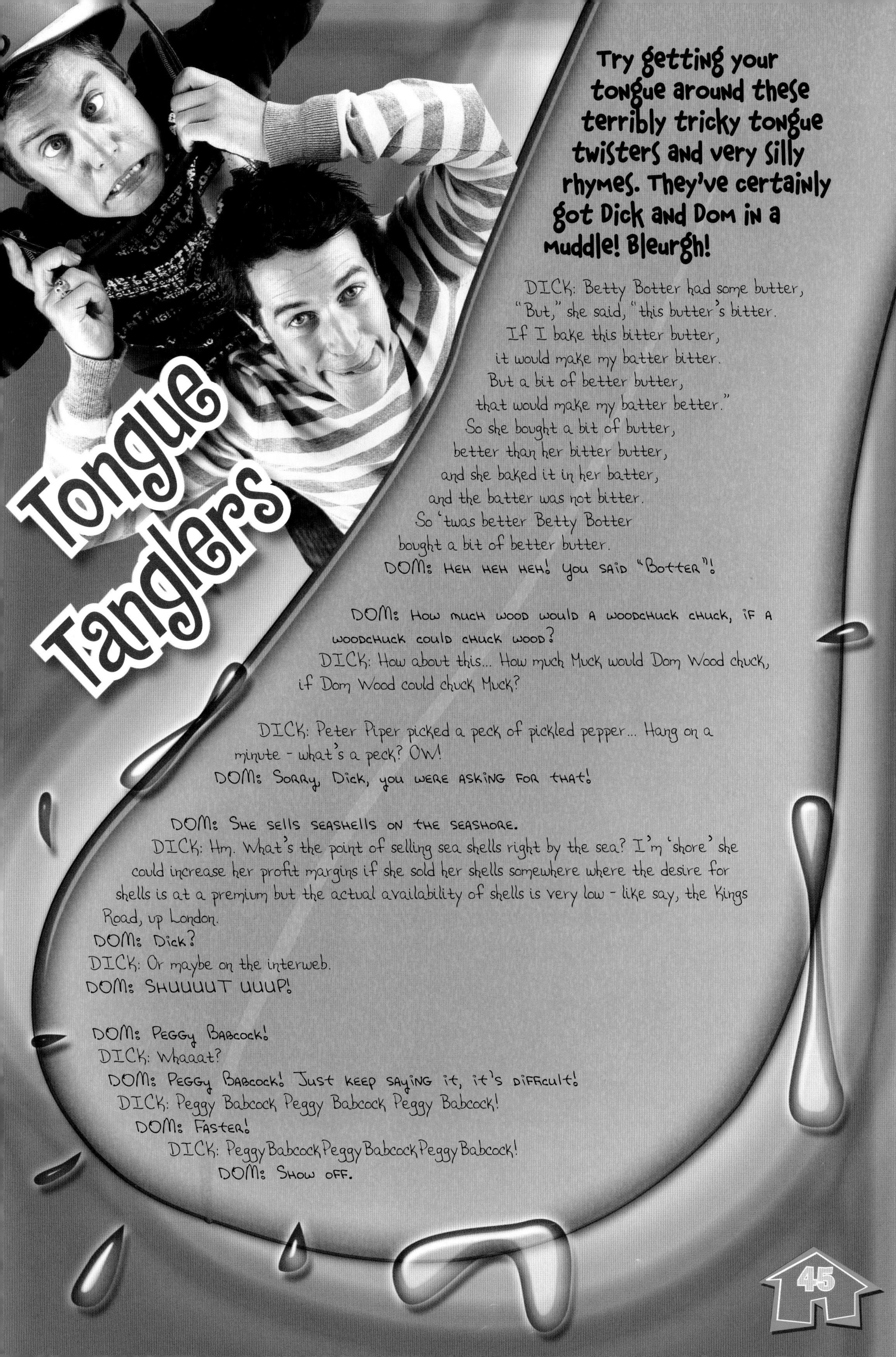

Tongue Tanglers

Try getting your tongue around these terribly tricky tongue twisters and very silly rhymes. They've certainly got Dick and Dom in a muddle! Bleurgh!

DICK: Betty Botter had some butter,
"But," she said, "this butter's bitter.
If I bake this bitter butter,
it would make my batter bitter.
But a bit of better butter,
that would make my batter better."
So she bought a bit of butter,
better than her bitter butter,
and she baked it in her batter,
and the batter was not bitter.
So 'twas better Betty Botter
bought a bit of better butter.

DOM: HEH HEH HEH! You said "Botter"!

DOM: How much wood would a woodchuck chuck, if a woodchuck could chuck wood?

DICK: How about this... How much Muck would Dom Wood chuck, if Dom Wood could chuck Muck?

DICK: Peter Piper picked a peck of pickled pepper... Hang on a minute - what's a peck? OW!

DOM: Sorry, Dick, you were asking for that!

DOM: She sells seashells on the seashore.

DICK: Hm. What's the point of selling sea shells right by the sea? I'm 'shore' she could increase her profit margins if she sold her shells somewhere where the desire for shells is at a premium but the actual availability of shells is very low - like say, the Kings Road, up London.

DOM: Dick?

DICK: Or maybe on the interweb.

DOM: SHUUUUT UUUP!

DOM: Peggy Babcock!

DICK: Whaaat?

DOM: Peggy Babcock! Just keep saying it, it's difficult!

DICK: Peggy Babcock Peggy Babcock Peggy Babcock!

DOM: Faster!

DICK: PeggyBabcockPeggyBabcockPeggyBabcock!

DOM: Show off.

Dick & Dom's TV Choice

If Dick and Dom had control of your remote for the day, here's the kind of programmes they would make you watch...

DTV 1

6.00 **Dick and Dom in da Bungalow.** 12 hour Muckathon. See TV Choice!

6.00 **The Stimpsons.** Jay Cat invents a machine to make Wren happy.

6.30 **Hollyhocks.** Johnny and Amanda resolve their marital dispute by playing a game of conkers.

7.00 **News.** New lamps for old.

8.00 **Look At That Floater.** Historian Bald Rick looks at what may have happened if the Titanic hadn't sunk.

9.00 **Pull My Finger.** New game show presented by Vernon Jay.

10.00 **TV Out-takes part 609.** More shelf-falling-down, line-forgetting, door-knob-coming-off howlers.

10.45 **It Came From Widnes!** Late night movie hi-jinx

12.35 **Ernest.** Very long movie starring Kevin Costly and Tom Hanky.

4.50 **Close.** Told you it was long!

DTV 2

6.00 **Kiddyland!** It's twinkle time in Kiddyland!

6.15 **Birthdays!** Let's hope you woke up in time!

6.30 **Hurrah!**

6.35 **Ballyhoo!**

6.45 **Toasty** – the biggest cheese toasty in the world! More snack-based malarkey!

7.00 **Kids!** Love! Exclamation! Marks! Alright! They sure do!

7.05 **Breakfast News.** News.

7.30 **Breakfast News.** For those who got up a bit later.

9.00 **Mid-morning News.**

10.00 **Late morning News.**

11.00 **Elevenses News.**

11.55 **News Round-up.** Round-up of news.

12.00 **Lunchtime News.** What people are having for lunch around the world...

12.30 **Regional variation.** ...and across your region.

1.00 **"Murder!" She Screamed.** Triple bill.

4.00 **Changing Attics.** Bill from Bedford swaps his attic for a cellar.

5.00 **I'm A Schoolboy, Get Me Out Of Here!** The kids are up to their knees in it, upside down.

5.30 **Teacher Swap.**

6.00 **I'm A Schoolboy, Get Me Out Of Here!** Live Challenge. Study those bugs, don't eat them!

7.00 **Teacher Swap Changed Our School.**

8.00 **House Swap.**

9.00 **Toy Swap.** Nikki from Manchester gets a Dick and Dom DVD for a packet of Top of the Pops Top Trumps with one of Westlife missing.

10.00 **Swap Swap.** Two people who swapped jobs swap swaps with two people who swapped holidays and then swap snaps.

11.00 **Pet Swap.**

12.00 **Kid Swap.**

1.00 **Swab Swap.** Live from St. James's Hospital.

2.00 **Telly Swap.** Can I swap mine for one with something else on?

- **Ashamed by your girly hands?**
- **Look like you've never done an honest day's graft?**
- **Choose... Fingernail Dirt!**

Join the likes of TV's *Lawrence Lally-Boyo* and *Alan Bigbog* and have your own glamorously dirty fingernails! You don't need to attend premieres and award ceremonies to convince others that you have done an honest day's toil, just use our patented fingernail dirt recipe!

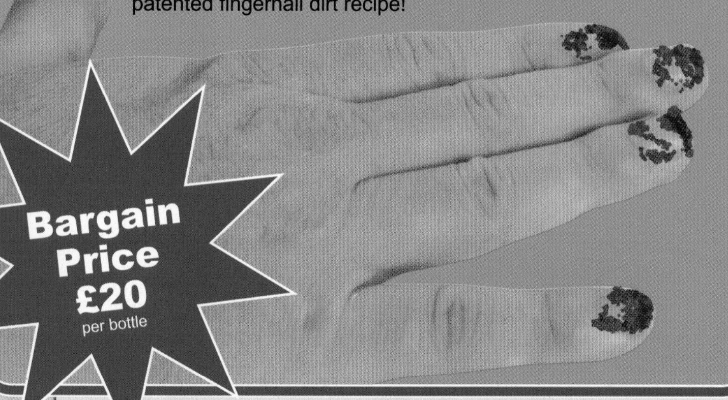

DICK & DOM'S TV CHOICE

Dick and Dom in da Bungalow
6.00am DTV1

An epic 12 hours of top class entertainment, from the makers of Titanic (the boat, not the movie). Dick and Dom attempt to sink da Bungalow under a sea of Muck Muck and Dirty Norris. Luckily a floppy haired milksop by the curious name of Tom Dickunharry comes aboard to save the day. Does Tom have the nous to drag Dick and Dom out of the maelstrom before the ratings sink?

Regional

6.00 **Schools.**

12.00 **School's out.**

12.30 **School's back in!**

1.00 **I'm Buying A House.** Congratulations.

1.45 **I'm Buying A House – Abroad!** What do you want a medal?

2.30 **I'm A Celebrity! And I'm Buying A House Abroad!** Oh, for goodness sake.

3.15 **Countup.** More conundrums in the doldrums with your otherwise unemployable host, Richard Voderwoman.

4.00 **Bob The Estate Agent.** More larks with the jolly Estate Agent who's always ready to help you buy a house!

4.15 **My Parents are Bank Managers.** More anarchic comedy with the crazy family who love to save so they can buy a bigger house.

5.00 **Help! I'm A Teenage Nobody.** Teenagers who can't sing, dance or act. Hurrah!

6.00 **Teatime news.** Milk and two sugars, please. Oh, and one of those, please. Thanks.

7.00 **Westenders.** Cheryl goes up East. Butch sorts it out. A nice cuppa tea. Pint in the Albert.

7.30 **How Clean Is Your Bedroom?** Mu-u-um! Tell him he's not allowed in here, it's MY room!

8.15 **No!** The show no celebrities can say the title of.

9.00 **Undercover report.** The truth about Britain's school dinners, they stink.

10.00 **That's it.**

11.00 **No really.**

12.00 **I'm telling you.**

1.00 **Go to bed now!**

The Other Channel

6.00 **The Magazine Programme.** This week's topic – 'the'.

10.00 **Trashy** "My cattle won't go to market!"

11.00 **Trashy** "My buns don't rise as well as hers next door!"

12.00 **Trashy** "You're dumped! For a newer model (of earth moving machine)!"

1.00 **Ready Steady Burn.** Extended lunchtime special.

5.00 **Ready Steady Microwave.** With lunch ruined, I may be in need of something quick.

5.30 **Animal Police Kennel.** New docusoap – police pooches lay down the paw in a busy city centre police station.

6.00 **Pet Makeover.** Jim from Essex gets his guard poodle made over as a rottweiler.

7.00 **How Clean Is Your Pet in the Attic?** And can you get a tenner for it?

8.00 **Something presented by someone called Johnny.** Chance your luck by tuning in.

9.00 **Hard lines.** Children spell it out to the grown-ups "T-V I-S B-O-R-I-N-G."

10.00 **Football – forever.** And hardly ever any other sport. By royal decree.

Limp, dull and lifeless hair?
Look lively with Creamy Muck Muck!

Magic Muck Muck works five ways on your hair!

1. Reflective fructoils make your hair bling.
2. Active isotopes deeply penetrate the shafts of your hair to condition it from within.
3. Twinkle Stick applicator keeps your hair pointing north at all times – even when snorkelling.
4. Drives the getaway car in a bungled heist movie.
5. Tastes nice!

Don't be a loser all your life – dunk your head in a bucket of Muck!

Dick or Dom? or the Prize Idiot??

Do you like Dick? Or are you a friend of Dom? Follow this flow chart to find out who would be your best friend in da Bungalow – Dick, Dom...or the Prize Idiot!

The ^really Serious Page

You probably didn't know this, but Dick and Dom are actually very serious, intelligent and respectable men. Yes, above all – men! All that boyish mucking about is just a clever act. Seriously! Which is why they are able to answer the brain tangling questions here. Did I mention this was serious?

Q: Why is the sky blue?

A: Ah, a frequently asked question! But you won't get the answer from lying on your back in the park among the dewy grass, the dinky little daisies and other such unmanly things! No! Like so many other conundrums you will find the answer in science! The sky is blue simply because if it was green or brown or grey it would be confused with land and we'd keep walking off into it. And we couldn't have that, could we? No. Safe to say – if it's blue it's the sky. Or the sea. Or a very rum shop with blue carpet. Either way – don't step into it!

Q: Why doesn't glue stick to the inside of the tube?

A: Because the inside of a tube of glue is not sticky!

Q: How do they get the flavour into bubbly gum?

A: Your so-called 'bubbly gum,' is the scourge of modern society – dalmationing our streets with nasty black spots! I will answer your question so long as you dispose of your gum responsibly! OK, the flavour in bubbly gum is transferred from the chosen fruit – strawberry, gumberry or mint leaf – using a special transference ray that was invented by the BBC for episode 83 of Doctor Who ("Help, Doctor! I Switched Bodies!" – 1979). The fruit is smothered in cooking oil and zapped by the Ray Ray Ray (named after it's inventor – Ray Raymonde) that transfers the flavour of the whole fruit into tablets of gum. The virtually flavourless fruit is then sold on to low rent supermarkets.

Q: Why do I close my eyes when I sneeze?

A: You've seen what comes out of a nose. It's not nice. Why would you want to see it? Mother Nature has some decorum and I'd thank you to have some too.

Q: If the Earth is spinning, how come I don't just fly off into space?

A: Believe it or not, we're all – all of us, women and girls included – covered in microscopic creatures. We like to think that we're clean and antiseptic – but we're not, not entirely. You see, there are creatures in our eyelashes, in our hair and – most of all – there are creatures clinging on to the soles of our feet. These tiny, helpful creatures – known as Clingons – are what keep us fixed to this wonderful planet as it hurtles precariously through space. Clingons are nature's own Velcro – so think of them with every step you take and tread carefully as you make your way through life. Don't lose your grip and don't let rip.

Q: Why doesn't our moon have a name?

A: It does – but it's called Jemima and that's a big girl's name so we scientists just call it 'The Moon,' as it sounds manlier. I mean, Neil Armstrong, the first man to set foot on Jemima? Wrong, wrong, wrong!

Q: Is it true that every time you drink a glass of water you are drinking some of the same molecules that have passed through our very own Queen?

A: No.

BODY TALK

Ever wanted to know what a mate is trying to tell you – even when they're too shy to say it? Or maybe they're not going to say something, but they're THINKING it! Well now you can read peoples' minds – merely by looking at their bodies!

I wish I hadn't had that extra bean burrito at lunch.
I think no-one's looking at me.
I wish I'd got a budgerigar instead of that dog.
I wish I'd got a dog instead of that budgerigar.

PANTS DANCE

I got my head in my pants
(I wouldn't believe it 'less I'd seen it)
I'm in a groovy disco trance
(Are you sure that that's hygenic?)
They were clean on just last week
(Good grief they're going to reek)
yeh, yeh baby look at me!

I've gotta dance in my pants
Just like they do in France
you gotta take a chance
And do the knickers on your noodle prance

And dance in your pants!

DICK'S GUIDE TO COMEDY

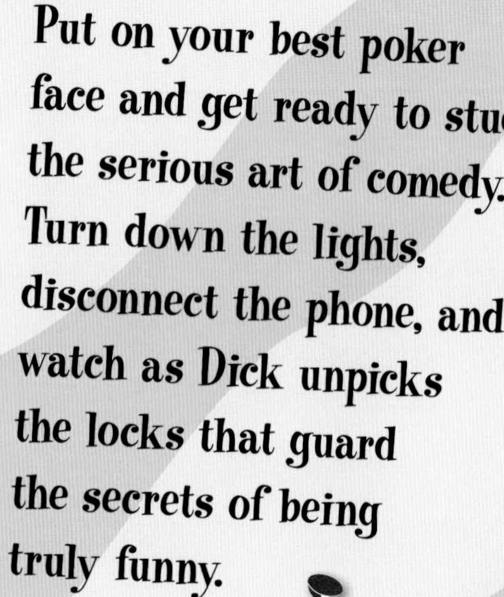

Put on your best poker face and get ready to study the serious art of comedy. Turn down the lights, disconnect the phone, and watch as Dick unpicks the locks that guard the secrets of being truly funny.

Dick's top 10 comedy meat products!

Just insert any of these savoury foodstuffs into a sentence for guaranteed laughs. (Unless you're talking to a vegetarian like Dom, the wuss.)

Manky sausage
Meat pie
Haggis
Saveloy
Chipolata
Scotch egg
Kebab
Thick onion gravy
Frankfurter
Whole uncooked chicken

Dick's top 10 comedy clothing items!

A quick review of British cinema is all it takes to reaffirm the intrinsic comedy value of a big pair of lady pants! But there is more to comedy than undercrackers - there's tights as well!

A pair of tights
A bonnet
Big lady pants
Y-fronts
Stinky socks
Suspenders - especially sock suspenders
Braces - or, as the Americans call them... suspenders!
Galoshes
Culottes
Shoes that are too big (unless they're your new school shoes and then that's not funny, just optimistic)

Dick's 10 best things to say after burping!

There's nothing like a can of fizzy pop to unleash the gas beast within. But what to say when you silence the room with a real lip trembler?

"More tea vicar?"
"Now let's see who the burpatrator REALLY is..."
"I could chew on that one!"
"And for the rest of today's news..."
"Burple always was my favourite colour."
"Another cream horn, vicar?"
"I'm sure THAT one had legs."
"Come in!"
"Oooh, these mobile ringtones are so vulgar these days, are they not?"
"Thank you and good night."

BRAAARP!

Dick's 10 best places to play Bogies!

Not much gets me stifling a titter as much as a good old-fashioned game of Bogies! But the arena in which you choose to play the game is crucial - so here are my favourite places to yell "Bogies!"

The library
A bus queue
A museum
Your Dad's office
The staffroom
A golf course
Clothes shop changing rooms
On a train
In a lift
At a yoga class

DOM'S DIARY

You asked for it, and you got it! No, not a pony...or a new bike...but a sneaky peek inside Dom's diary! Get inside the head of one of Britain's greatest thinkers with these pages torn directly from the secret scribblings of Dominic Wood aged 13 and a bit.

Monday

A hard day's work trying to dream up great new games for our top-rated TV show - for Dick. Meanwhile, I went shopping.
Went to the supermarket to buy food but ended up getting drawn into a bogies tournament. It was a toughie, but I pulled it off. And once I'd wrestled that bogey out of my nose, I went to get my shopping.
Unfortunately, I didn't have a pound coin for the trolley so I had to get some change.
Went to the games shop and bought a new computer game and an extra controller for Dick. Totally forgot about the shopping, but man can live for three days without food or water so long as he still hasn't reached the final level of his new game. Or so I heard. Decided to test that theory.

Tuesday

I don't know about three days. One night was long enough before we cracked and ordered pizza for breakfast.
Had to be very patient with Dick. It took him a long time to learn all his special moves for the game. I left the room once and, when I came back, he still hadn't beaten me. Dick said it was like patting your tummy and rubbing your head at the same time.
Decided to play something far less challenging and so retired to the library for a game of Bogies!
Dick had some strange idea of looking at books. What does he think libraries are for? I kicked the game off with a 3.2 and was on a roll from that point on. I was halfway through a 9.8 when we got thrown out of the library. We had a big argument then about whether it counts if you don't let out a whole "bogies".
Went home for a cup of tea and a sit down in front of the TV. There was nothing on, so I got up and plugged it in. Watched TV all night. Sleep is a con!

Wednesday

Amazing what they have on TV these days. We've got a vase of plastic flowers and a toy trumpet.
Amazing how many new ways I can discover to annoy Dick. The toy trumpet worked a treat! I won't tell you what I did with the plastic flowers.

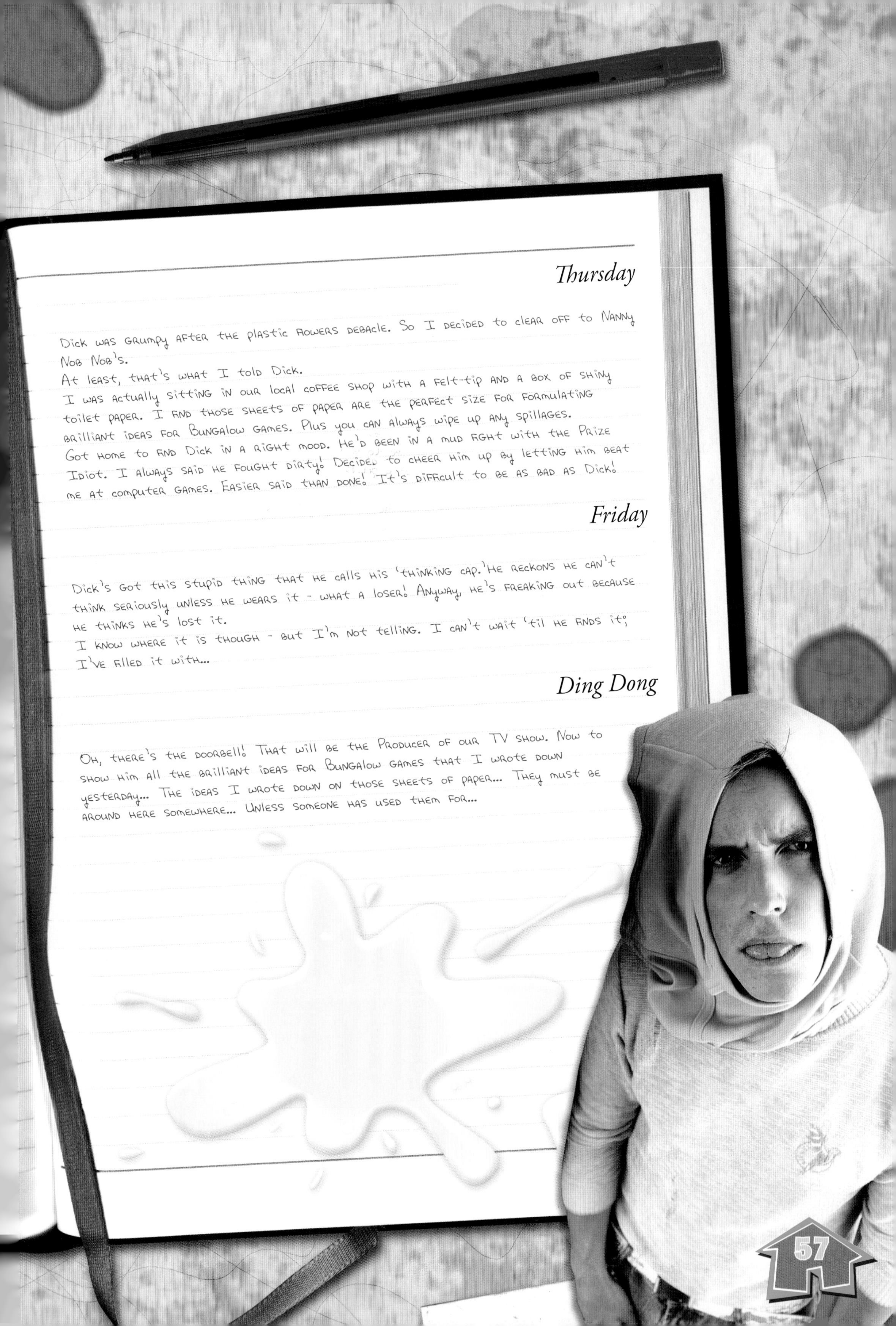

Thursday

Dick was grumpy after the plastic flowers debacle. So I decided to clear off to Nanny Nob Nob's.
At least, that's what I told Dick.
I was actually sitting in our local coffee shop with a felt-tip and a box of shiny toilet paper. I find those sheets of paper are the perfect size for formulating brilliant ideas for Bungalow Games. Plus you can always wipe up any spillages.
Got home to find Dick in a right mood. He'd been in a mud fight with the Prize Idiot. I always said he fought dirty! Decided to cheer him up by letting him beat me at computer games. Easier said than done! It's difficult to be as bad as Dick!

Friday

Dick's got this stupid thing that he calls his 'thinking cap.' He reckons he can't think seriously unless he wears it - what a loser! Anyway, he's freaking out because he thinks he's lost it.
I know where it is though - but I'm not telling. I can't wait 'til he finds it; I've filled it with...

Ding Dong

Oh, there's the doorbell! That will be the Producer of our TV show. Now to show him all the brilliant ideas for Bungalow Games that I wrote down yesterday... The ideas I wrote down on those sheets of paper... They must be around here somewhere... Unless someone has used them for...

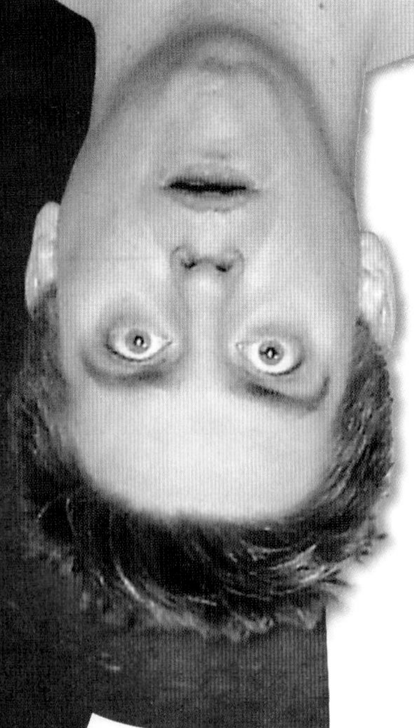

Dick & Dom's Playtime

Dick has written a play, luvvie! And if he can do it, so can you! Here's a short extract from his magnum opus (that means he wrote it on the back of ten ice cream bar wrappers). Have a look at it, and see if you can't come up with something better. It shouldn't be too difficult.

Dick's top tips for making a successful debut in the theatre.

Remember – plays aren't just about words! Your play should be full of action! Cram in as many scenes involving buckets of Creamy Muck Muck as you can and you'll have your audience eating out of your hands (so make sure you wash them before the show!)

Nothing is so bad it can't be covered with make-up. You should see Dom in the morning before he puts on his panstick. No, actually, no one except his Mum should see that. Seriously, though, no one will notice any holes in your plot if you appear on stage wearing enough make-up. The basic rule about make-up is this – too much is not enough!

Step into the light! If it's too dark – they can't see you! It's very important – especially in comedy – that everyone can see your face. That's why no one ever laughs while listening to the radio.

When staging your play, you don't have to think big! You could act it out with puppets! And, if you use finger puppets, you don't even need to employ any other actors – after all, that's ten possible characters you have right there in your hands! So, come on! Get that biro out and go for it!

The Earnestness of Being Important

By Richard McCourt

The persons of the pla

Hon. Richard McCourt
Rev. Dominic Wood
Sandwich, Manservant
Lady Nob Nob
Cecily Yours, Governess
Boris McSquirter

Time: the present
Place: London Town

ACT FIRST

Scene: Saturday morning room in da Bungalow. The room is artistically and luxuriously furnished – if a little mucky. The sound of a stylophone is heard in the adjoining room. Sandwich is arranging buckets of Creamy Muck Muck on the table and, after the music ceases, McCourt enters.

McCourt: Did you hear what I was playing, Sandwich?
Sandwich: I thought it impolite to listen, sir. Although it sounded wonderful.
McCourt: It was The Ride of the Valkyries – on the stylophone.
Sandwich: Very good, sir.
McCourt: Wasn't it? Now, have you the cheese sandwiches ready for Lady Nob Nob?
Sandwich: Oh, yes!
McCourt: And the buckets of Creamy Muck Muck?
Sandwich: Right here. Would you like one, sir?
McCourt: Not yet, Sandwich, not yet.
Sandwich: I can recommend the cheese sandwiches, sir. They're most delicious at this time of year.
McCourt (languidly): I don't believe I am much interested in your thoughts regarding the time of year, Sandwich.
[He takes a sandwich and fills his face. Enter Wood.]
Sandwich: The Reverend Wood.
Wood: What, ho!
McCourt: My dear, Dominic! What brings you up to town?
Wood: Ah, the Muck! The Muck! What else should bring one anywhere? Eating, as usual Dicky, darling?
McCourt (stiffly): I believe it is customary to partake of spoils at this time. May I interest you in some Creamy Muck Muck?
Wood: After you, luvvie!
McCourt: Don't mind if I do!
[McCourt flings a bucket of Creamy Muck Muck over Rev. Wood.]
Wood: Hurrah!
[Rev. Wood lobs a bucket of Creamy Muck Muck over McCourt.]
McCourt: I say!
[McCourt chucks a bucket of Creamy Muck Muck over Rev. Wood.]
Wood: Jolly good!
[Rev. Wood hurls a bucket of Creamy Muck Muck over McCourt.]
McCourt: Wa-hey!
[Lady Nob Nob enters.]
Lady Nob Nob: Richard!
McCourt: Lady Nob Nob!
Wood: Crikey!

Now let the muse take over, and write the rest of the play! What could happen next? Does the rest of the Creamy Muck Muck stay in the buckets? Or does Lady Nob Nob get it in the face? Does Sandwich ever get a sandwich? Who goes? You decide!

Da wisdom of da ancients

Now we're reaching the beginning of the end of the book, we have to ask ourselves, "What have we learned...?" The answer is probably, "Not much." But, luckily, old Mr McCourt and stinky Mr Wood are here to dispense the wisdom of the sum of all their years!

Never eat yellow snow.

May your life be like toilet paper – long and useful.

It never rains but actions speak louder than moss.

Education is a brilliant thing – it's wasted on kids.

Always smile – it makes everyone wonder what you're up to.

A stitch in the bird must come down.

I used to be conceited – but now I'm perfect!

Most of a dog's mistakes are made by its 'faux pas.'

Don't let worry kill you – let counselling help.

Advice – the one thing it's easier to give than to receive.

Look before many hands make light broth.

DICK: Dom, your good ideas are like diamonds.

DOM: Because they're so valuable?

DICK: No, because they're so rare.

AN EARLY BIRD IN THE HAND GATHERS LESS SPEED.
Don't count your chickens before you leap into the bush.

Far Out ~~Further~~ Reading

Remember – reading improves the mind! And I am the evidence because I have read all these books here! So if you have enjoyed our book, then perhaps you would like to take a look at some of the other titles here.

Everything Is All Around by Luke A. Round

Between Dom's Ears by M.T. Space

I've Just Let Off BY C.M. RUN

How To Answer Every Question and Never Be Wrong *by Ida Noh*

Inside the Tights: the Real Story Behind the Merry Men by Robin D. Rich

How To Read A Book Without Even Opening It **by Oz Moses**

THE TELEPHONE MESSAGE by Colin Bach

The Rules of Subtraction by Morris Les

Pfft...! Eurgh! *by Henrietta Moth*

Embarrassing Problem *by Lucy Lastic*

Don't Climb Trees by Anthony Pants

WHERE'S MY HOLE? by Phil Din

Chapel Hat Pegs *by Angus McCoatup*

The Whole Truth, And Nothing But by Laura Norda

Are you ready for school? *By S. Isa Cummin*

My True Life Adventure *by Paige Turner*

LONG DISTANCE LOVERS **by Miles A. Part**

The All Cabbage Diet by I. Malone

My Worst Week by Gladys Friday

Don't wake the Baby **by Elsie Cries**

Making Light Work of Your Problems ***by Linda Hand***

THE WORST JOURNEY IN THE WORLD by Helen Back

The All Meat Diet *by Lena Bacon*

Bungee Jumping For Babies by Hugo First Jnr.

The Fast Food Diet *by Caesar Salad*

THE BEGINNING OF THE END GAME
Leave da Bungalow – yes, go right outside – and yell "bogies!" as loud as you dare. The other Bungalowheads decide how loud you just shouted on a scale of 1-5 and then you can move forward that number!
Say something in a very high Diddy Dick and Dom voice. Move forward a diddy one.
Do your best impres- of the moose – BUUUR And then hop forw one.
FINISH!
Pretend you're making a bogey jelly. Give a running commentary on everything you do – and don't forget to describe how your jelly tastes! Move forward one.
Sometime between now and your next turn shout "Spam fritters," at the top of your voice! On your next turn, add the number of people who jumped to your throw of the dice.
Do the pants dance for thirty seconds, then move forward five!
Swap a sock with the person on your left and both move forward two.
62